True Things
(ADULTS ~~DON'T WANT~~ KIDS TO KNOW)

SEE WHAT PEOPLE ARE SAYING ABOUT Jimmy Gownley's AMELIA RULES!™

"Haven't read comics before? This is where you'll want to start."
—*Girls' Life*

"Perfectly captures the heartbreak, humor, and high drama of the middle school experience."
—Gene Yang, author of *American Born Chinese*

"Comic genius."
—GraphicNovelReporter.com

"I wish I could go back to middle school and make a friend like Amelia. I wish I could go back and *be* a friend like Amelia."
—the-trades.com

"So clever, smart, funny, and true. . . . This is one of the best graphic novel series out there for kids—and for adults with vivid, funny memories of childhood."
—Elizabeth Bluemle, the Flying Pig Bookstore

"One of the best cartoonists I know of, [Gownley] has never written a story that hasn't left me grinning madly."
—The Geeky Librarian

"Amelia Rules! remains my favorite graphic novel series for kids!"
—Tweendom.blogspot.com

"A Peanuts for the twenty-first century."
—*Comics Buyer's Guide*

"Simply one of the best all-ages comics I've ever seen."
—Mark Crilley, author/illustrator of the Akiko books

"Delightfully drawn and cleverly written."
—Orson Scott Card

"Side-splittingly hilarious. . . . Highly recommended for all ages and all libraries."
—*Library Journal*

"Full of wise-cracking jokes and quips, ingenious gags, screamingly funny dialogue, and the best of classic comic book antics."
—Megan McDonald, author of the Judy Moody series

"Amelia Rules! is . . . absolutely essential. Not only is it one of the finest comics of all time, it is one of the best examples of children's literature I have ever read."
—Kidz Corner Comic Reviews

"Smart and genuine."
—David Fury, writer/producer for *Lost,* and *Buffy the Vampire Slayer*

"Inspiring and uplifting in ways that will make you want to stand up and cheer. . . . Here's hoping the series continues for a good long time."
—the-trades.com

"Amelia's family and friends will take up permanent residence in your heart."
—Bob Schooley and Mark McCorkle, creators of Kim Possible

"Wonderful all-ages comic."
—*New York* magazine

"Gownley excels at putting a powerful message inside of a kid-friendly story."
—BSCKids.com

"Amelia Rules! . . . is a delightful entry for lovers of comics and realistic fiction. . . . She is a character to rival Ramona and Judy Moody."
—*School Library Journal*

"These kids are real . . . Gownley is a genius at capturing their perspective."
—ComicsWorthReading.com

MEET THE GANG

Amelia Louise McBride:
Our heroine. Wise cracking, yet sweet. She spends her time hanging out with friends and her aunt Tanner.

Reggie Grabinsky:
A.k.a. Captain Amazing. Founder of G.A.S.P., which he forces . . . er, encourages, his friends to join.

Rhonda Bleenie:
Smart, stubborn, and loud. She wears her heart on her sleeve and it's filled with love for Reggie.

Pajamaman:
Never speaks. Always cool. His feetie jammies tell you what's on his mind.

Tanner:
Amelia's aunt and a former rock 'n' roll superstar.

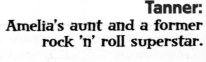

Amelia's Mom (Mary):
Starting a new life in Pennsylvania with Amelia after the divorce.

Amelia's Dad:
Still lives in New York, and
misses Amelia terribly.

G.A.S.P.
Gathering Of Awesome Super Pals.
The superhero club Reggie founded.

Park View Terrace Ninjas:
Club across town and nemesis
to G.A.S.P.

Kyle:
The main ninja. Kind of a jerk
but not without charm.

Joan:
Former Park View Terrace Ninja
(nemesis of G.A.S.P.), now friends
with Amelia and company.

Tweenie Zeenie: tweeniezeenie.com
A local kid-run magazine and Web site.

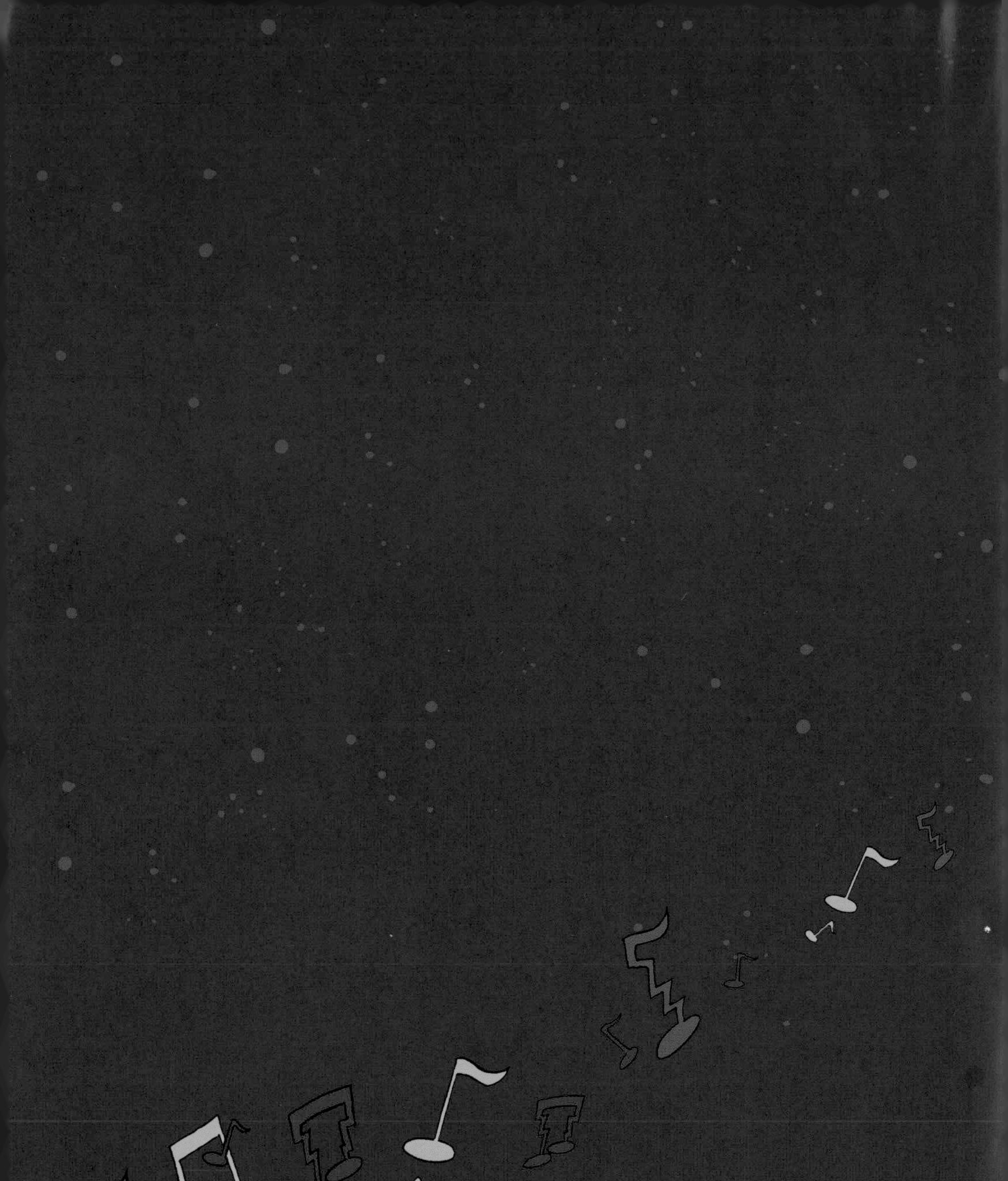

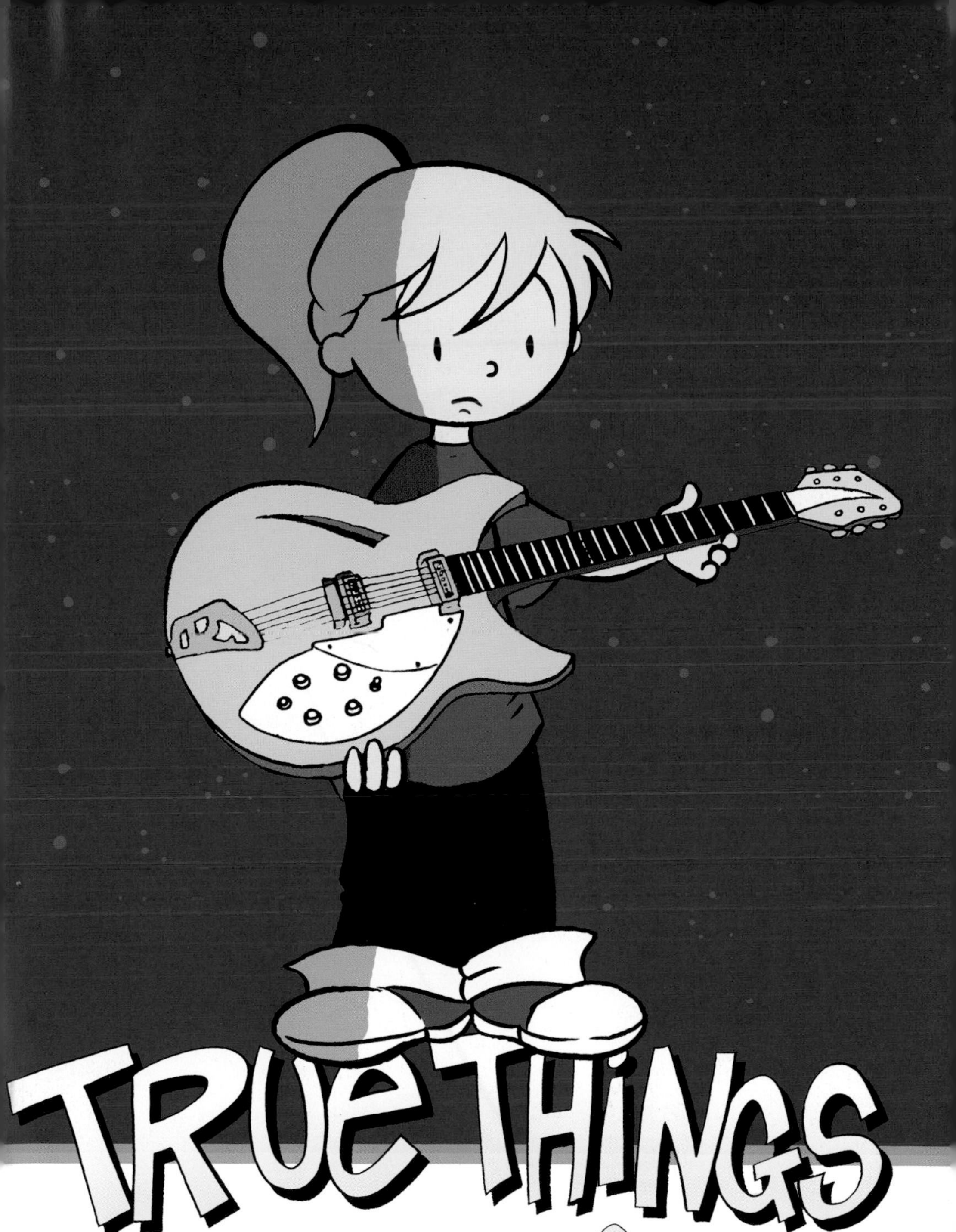

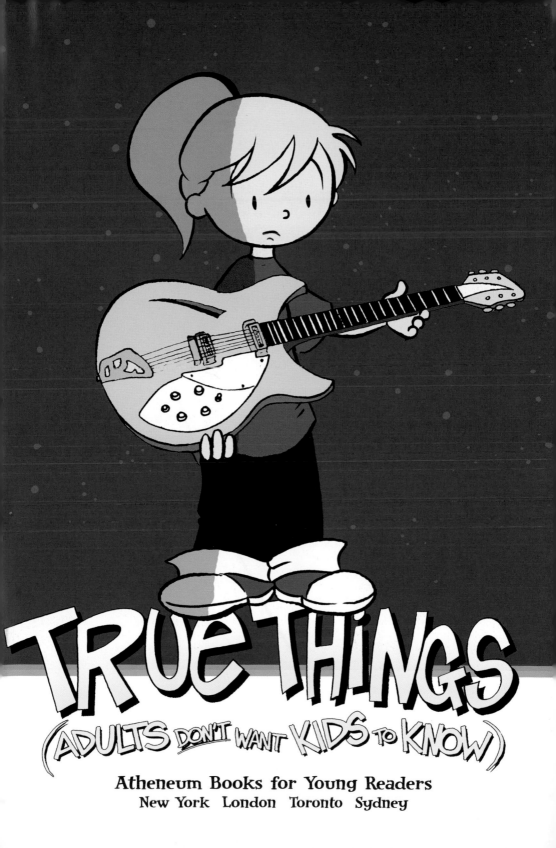

TRUE THINGS (ADULTS DON'T WANT KIDS TO KNOW)

Atheneum Books for Young Readers
New York London Toronto Sydney

For Karen Gownley,
who made the completion
of this book possible,
and for Ed Fox, Dan Almoney,
and Adam Wisniewski,
who never heard a crazy idea
they didn't like.

ATHENEUM BOOKS FOR YOUNG READERS
An imprint of Simon & Schuster Children's Publishing Division
1230 Avenue of the Americas, New York, New York 10020
This book is a work of fiction. Any references to historical events, real people,
or real locales are used fictitiously. Other names, characters, places, and incidents
are products of the author's imagination, and any resemblance to actual
events or locales or persons, living or dead, is entirely coincidental.
Copyright © 2010 by Jimmy Gownley
For information about special discounts for bulk purchases, please contact Simon & Schuster Special Sales
at 1-866-506-1949 or business@simonandschuster.com.
The Simon & Schuster Speakers Bureau can bring authors to your live event.
For more information or to book an event, contact the Simon & Schuster Speakers Bureau
at 1-866-248-3049 or visit our website at www.simonspeakers.com.
Also available in an Atheneum Books for Young Readers hardcover edition
Book design by Sonia Chaghatzbanian
The text for this book is hand-lettered.
The illustrations for this book are digitally rendered.
Manufactured in China
0716 SCP
6 8 10 9 7 5
Library of Congress Cataloging-in-Publication Data
Gownley, Jimmy.
True things : (adults don't want kids to know) / [by Jimmy Gownley]. — 1st ed.
p. cm. — (Jimmy Gownley's Amelia rules!)
Summary: Amelia Louise McBride's eleventh birthday party is fabulous, but soon her friends are
fighting all the time, she gets a terrible report card, and when she summons the courage to tell a
boy how she feels about him, she learns why it is called a "crush."
ISBN 978-1-4169-8611-9 (simultaneous hardcover) – ISBN 978-1-4169-8609-6 (simultaneous pbk.)
1. Graphic novels. [1. Graphic novels. 2. Schools—Fiction. 3. Popularity—Fiction. 4. Peer pressure—
Fiction. 5. Family life—Fiction.] I. Title.
PZ7.7.G69Tru 2010
741.5'973—dc22 2010007291

Jimmy Gownley's

AMELIA RULES!™

"The main difference between boys and
girls is that girls mature slightly
faster and boys are idiots."

–Tanner Clark
in an interview with
On the Scene magazine

CONNERTON,
POPULATION
2,100
Established 1832

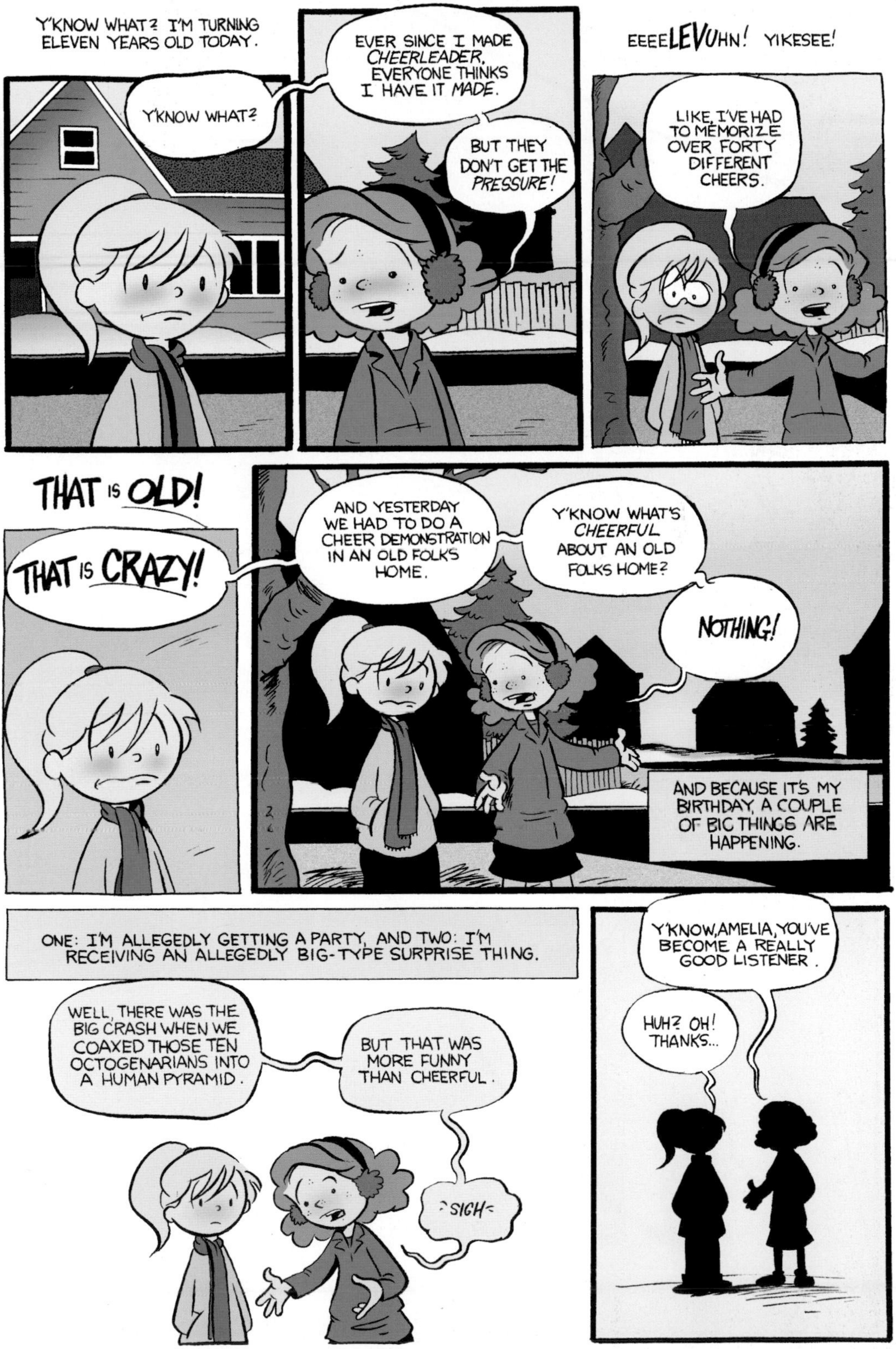
Y'KNOW WHAT? I'M TURNING ELEVEN YEARS OLD TODAY.
Y'KNOW WHAT?
EVER SINCE I MADE CHEERLEADER, EVERYONE THINKS I HAVE IT MADE.
BUT THEY DON'T GET THE PRESSURE!
EEEELEVUHN! YIKESEE!
LIKE, I'VE HAD TO MEMORIZE OVER FORTY DIFFERENT CHEERS.
THAT IS OLD!
THAT IS CRAZY!
AND YESTERDAY WE HAD TO DO A CHEER DEMONSTRATION IN AN OLD FOLKS HOME.
Y'KNOW WHAT'S CHEERFUL ABOUT AN OLD FOLKS HOME?
NOTHING!
AND BECAUSE IT'S MY BIRTHDAY, A COUPLE OF BIG THINGS ARE HAPPENING.
ONE: I'M ALLEGEDLY GETTING A PARTY, AND TWO: I'M RECEIVING AN ALLEGEDLY BIG-TYPE SURPRISE THING.
WELL, THERE WAS THE BIG CRASH WHEN WE COAXED THOSE TEN OCTOGENARIANS INTO A HUMAN PYRAMID.
BUT THAT WAS MORE FUNNY THAN CHEERFUL.
SIGH
Y'KNOW, AMELIA, YOU'VE BECOME A REALLY GOOD LISTENER.
HUH? OH! THANKS...

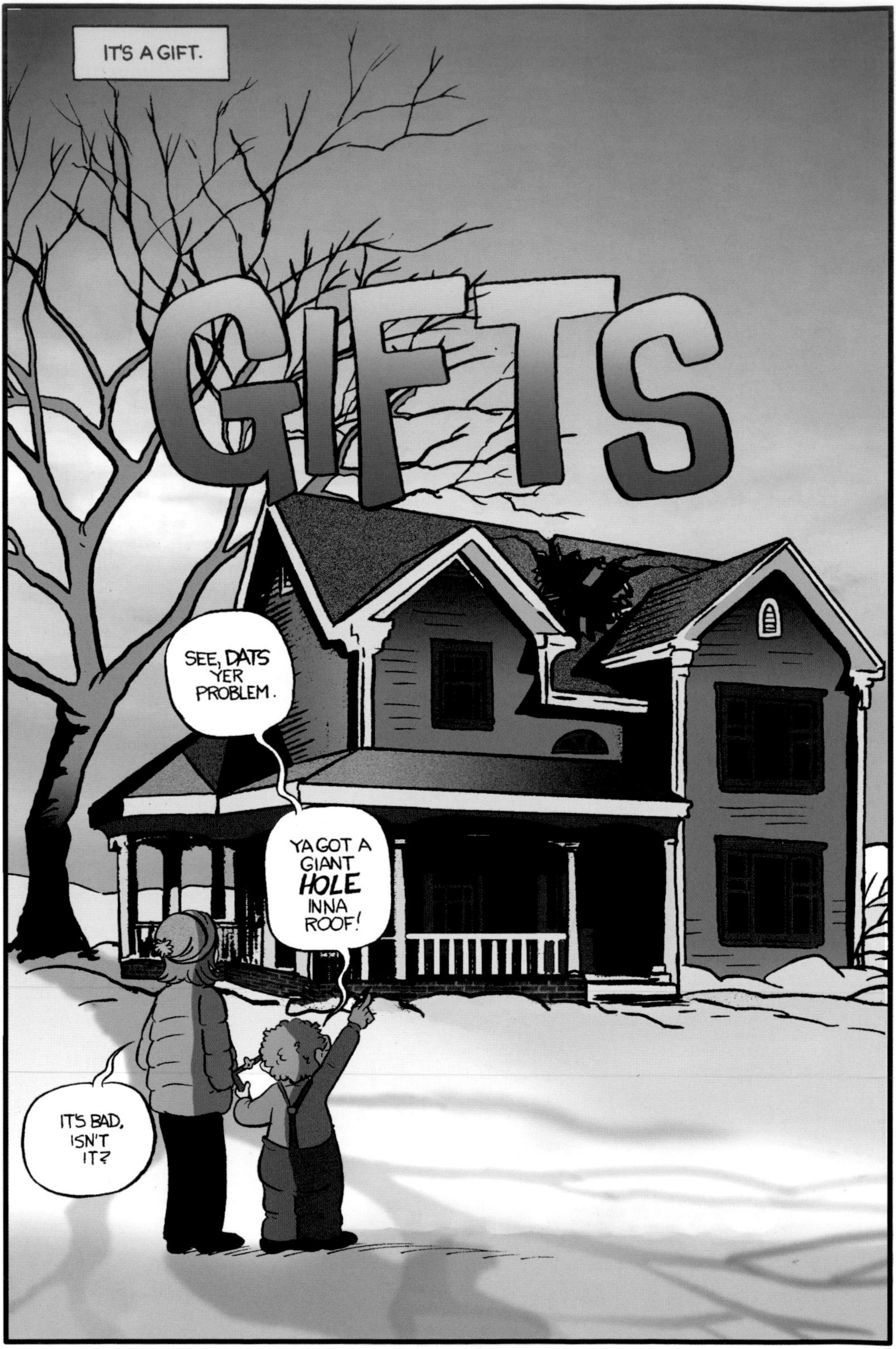
IT'S A GIFT.
GIFTS
SEE, DATS YER PROBLEM.
YA GOT A GIANT HOLE INNA ROOF!
IT'S BAD, ISN'T IT?

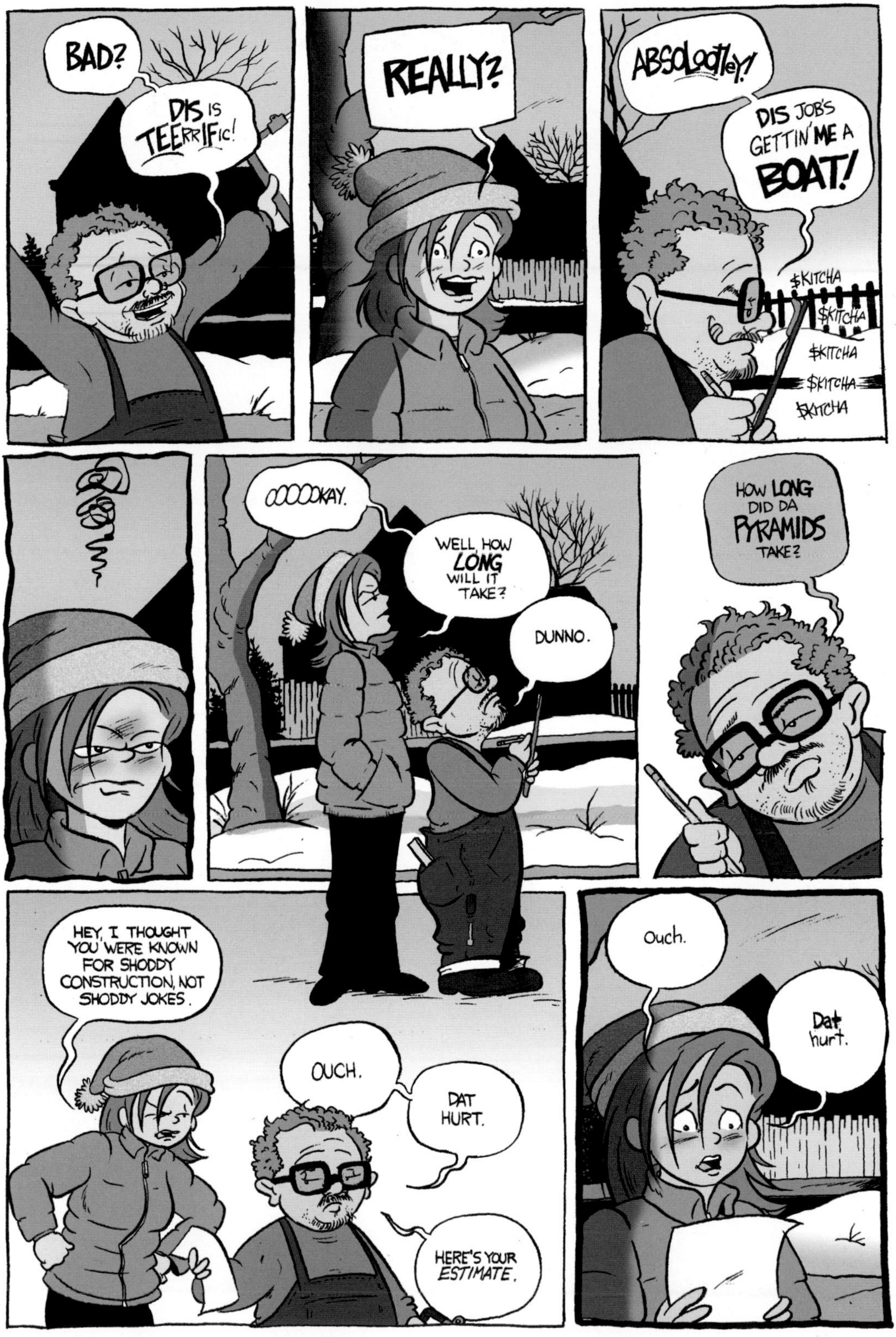
BAD?
DIS IS TEERRIFic!
REALLY?
ABSOLootley!
DIS JOB'S GETTIN' ME A BOAT!
$KITCHA
$KITCHA
$KITCHA
$KITCHA
$KITCHA
OOOOOKAY.
WELL, HOW LONG WILL IT TAKE?
DUNNO.
HOW LONG DID DA PYRAMIDS TAKE?
HEY, I THOUGHT YOU WERE KNOWN FOR SHODDY CONSTRUCTION, NOT SHODDY JOKES.
OUCH.
DAT HURT.
HERE'S YOUR ESTIMATE.
Ouch.
Dat hurt.

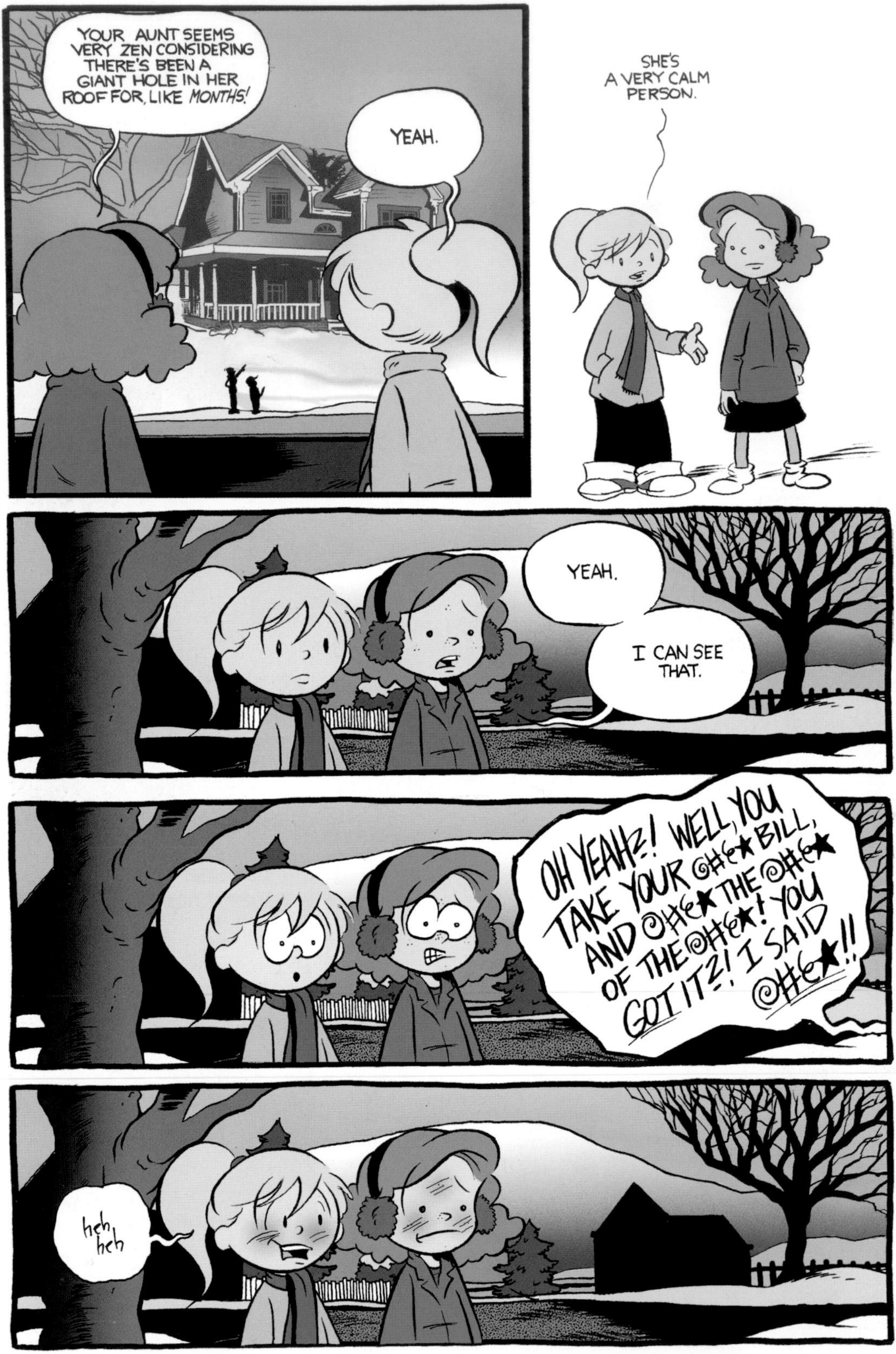
YOUR AUNT SEEMS VERY ZEN CONSIDERING THERE'S BEEN A GIANT HOLE IN HER ROOF FOR, LIKE MONTHS!
YEAH.
SHE'S A VERY CALM PERSON.
YEAH.
I CAN SEE THAT.
OH YEAH?! WELL, YOU TAKE YOUR @#€★ BILL, AND @#€★ THE @#€★ OF THE @#€★! YOU GOT IT?! I SAID @#€★!!
heh heh

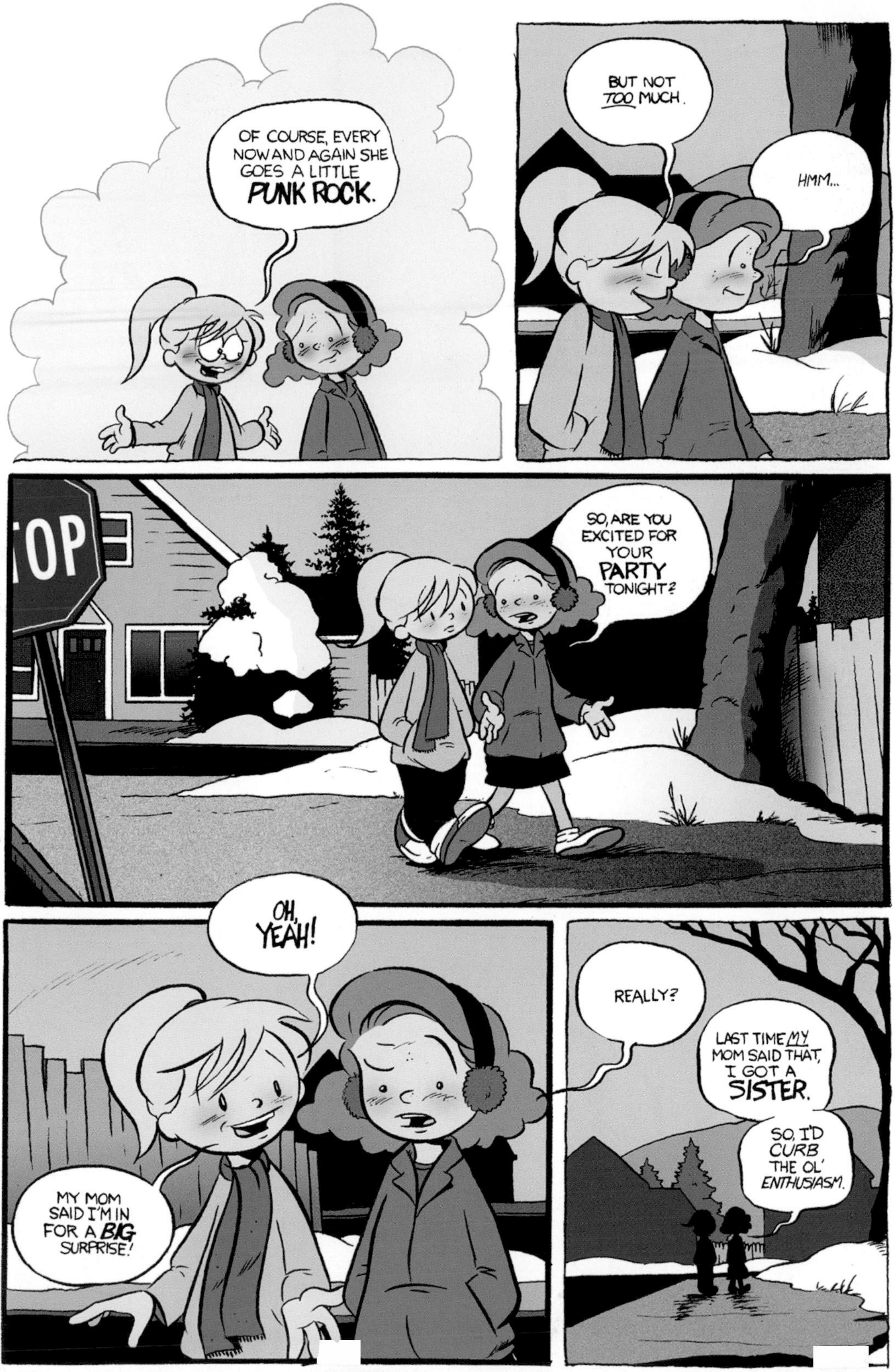

OF COURSE, EVERY NOW AND AGAIN SHE GOES A LITTLE PUNK ROCK.
BUT NOT TOO MUCH.
HMM...
TOP
SO, ARE YOU EXCITED FOR YOUR PARTY TONIGHT?
OH, YEAH!
MY MOM SAID I'M IN FOR A BIG SURPRISE!
REALLY?
LAST TIME MY MOM SAID THAT, I GOT A SISTER.
SO, I'D CURB THE OL' ENTHUSIASM.

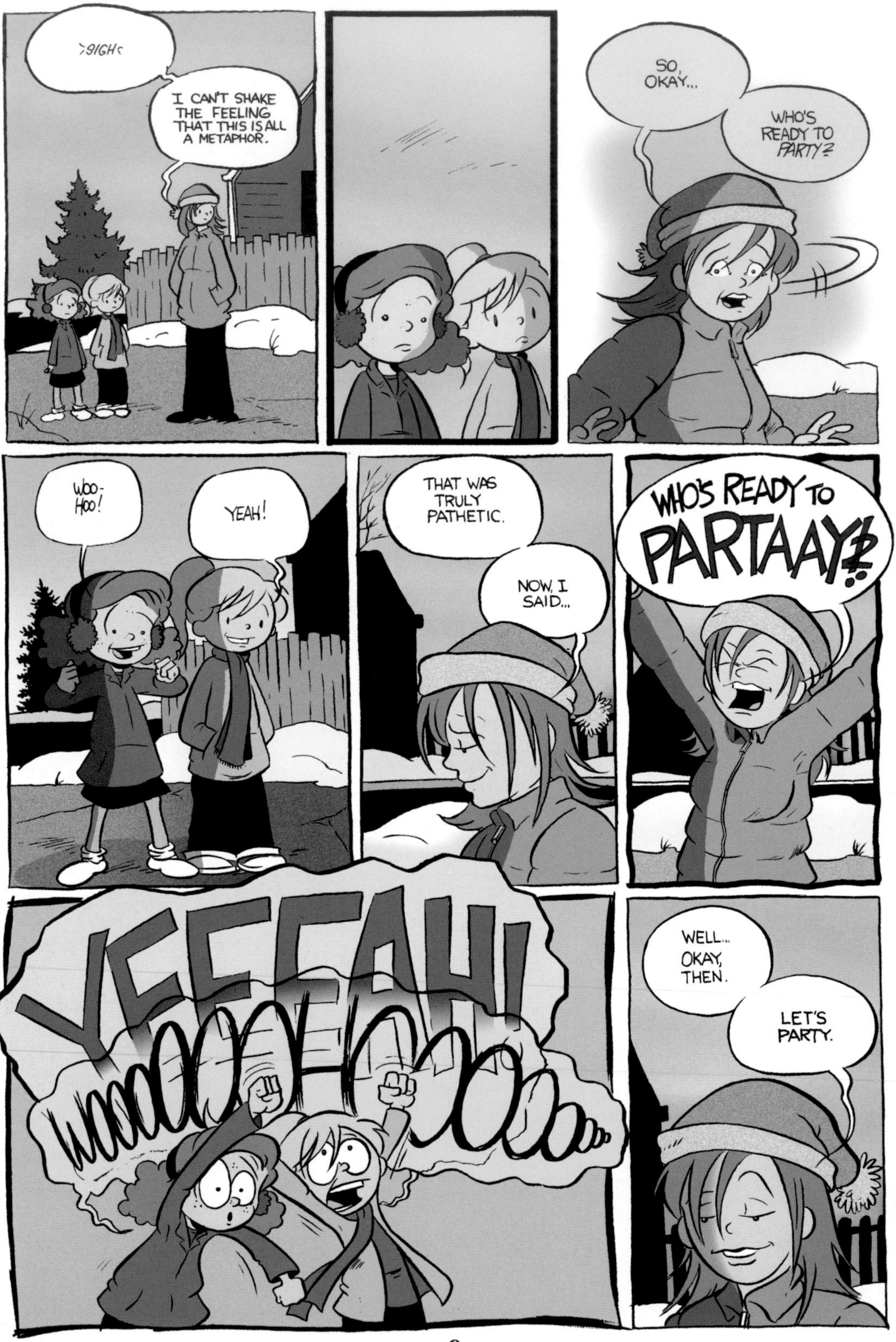
>SIGH<
I CAN'T SHAKE THE FEELING THAT THIS IS ALL A METAPHOR.
SO, OKAY...
WHO'S READY TO PARTY?!
WOO-HOO!
YEAH!
THAT WAS TRULY PATHETIC.
NOW, I SAID...
WHO'S READY TO PARTAAY?!
YEEEAH!
WOOOOOHOOOOO...
WELL... OKAY, THEN.
LET'S PARTY.

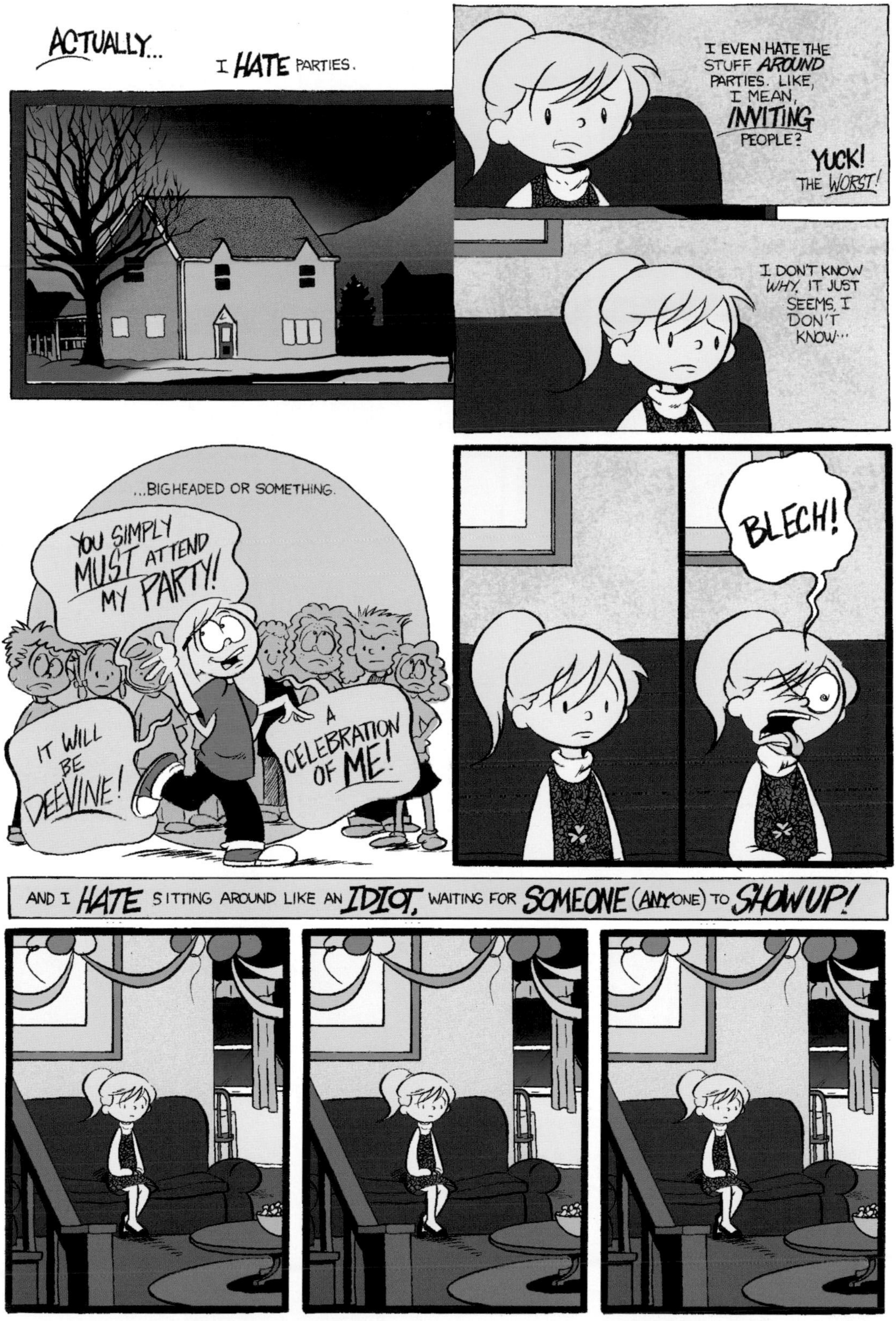
ACTUALLY...
I HATE PARTIES.
I EVEN HATE THE STUFF AROUND PARTIES. LIKE, I MEAN, INVITING PEOPLE?
YUCK! THE WORST!
I DON'T KNOW WHY. IT JUST SEEMS, I DON'T KNOW...
...BIGHEADED OR SOMETHING.
YOU SIMPLY MUST ATTEND MY PARTY!
IT WILL BE DEEVINE!
A CELEBRATION OF ME!
BLECH!
AND I HATE SITTING AROUND LIKE AN IDIOT, WAITING FOR SOMEONE (ANYONE) TO SHOW UP!

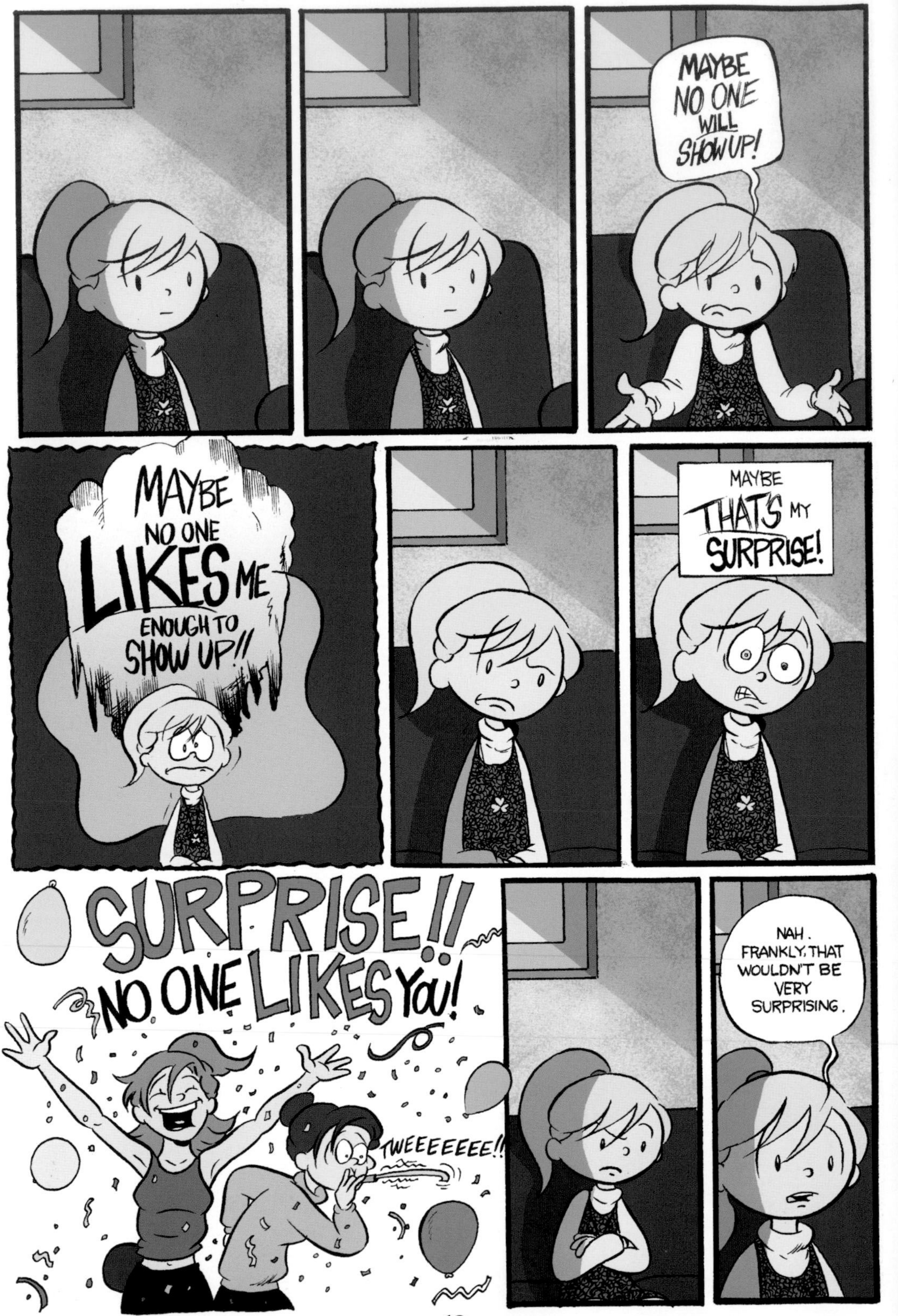
MAYBE NO ONE WILL SHOW UP!
MAYBE NO ONE LIKES ME ENOUGH TO SHOW UP!!
MAYBE THAT'S MY SURPRISE!
SURPRISE!! NO ONE LIKES YOU!
TWEEEEEEE!!
NAH. FRANKLY, THAT WOULDN'T BE VERY SURPRISING.

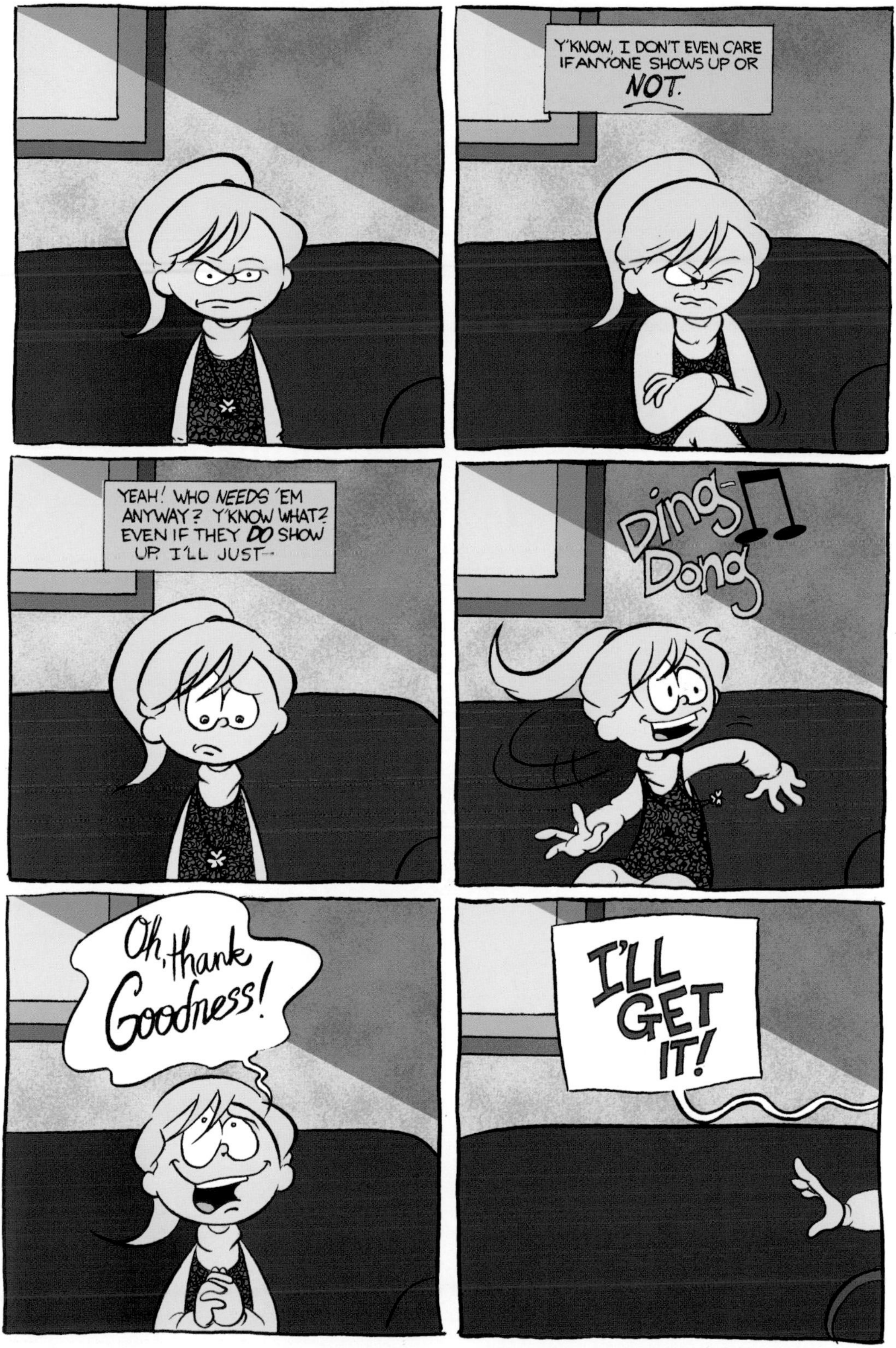
Y'KNOW, I DON'T EVEN CARE IF ANYONE SHOWS UP OR NOT.
YEAH! WHO NEEDS 'EM ANYWAY? Y'KNOW WHAT? EVEN IF THEY DO SHOW UP, I'LL JUST–
Ding-Dong
Oh, thank Goodness!
I'LL GET IT!

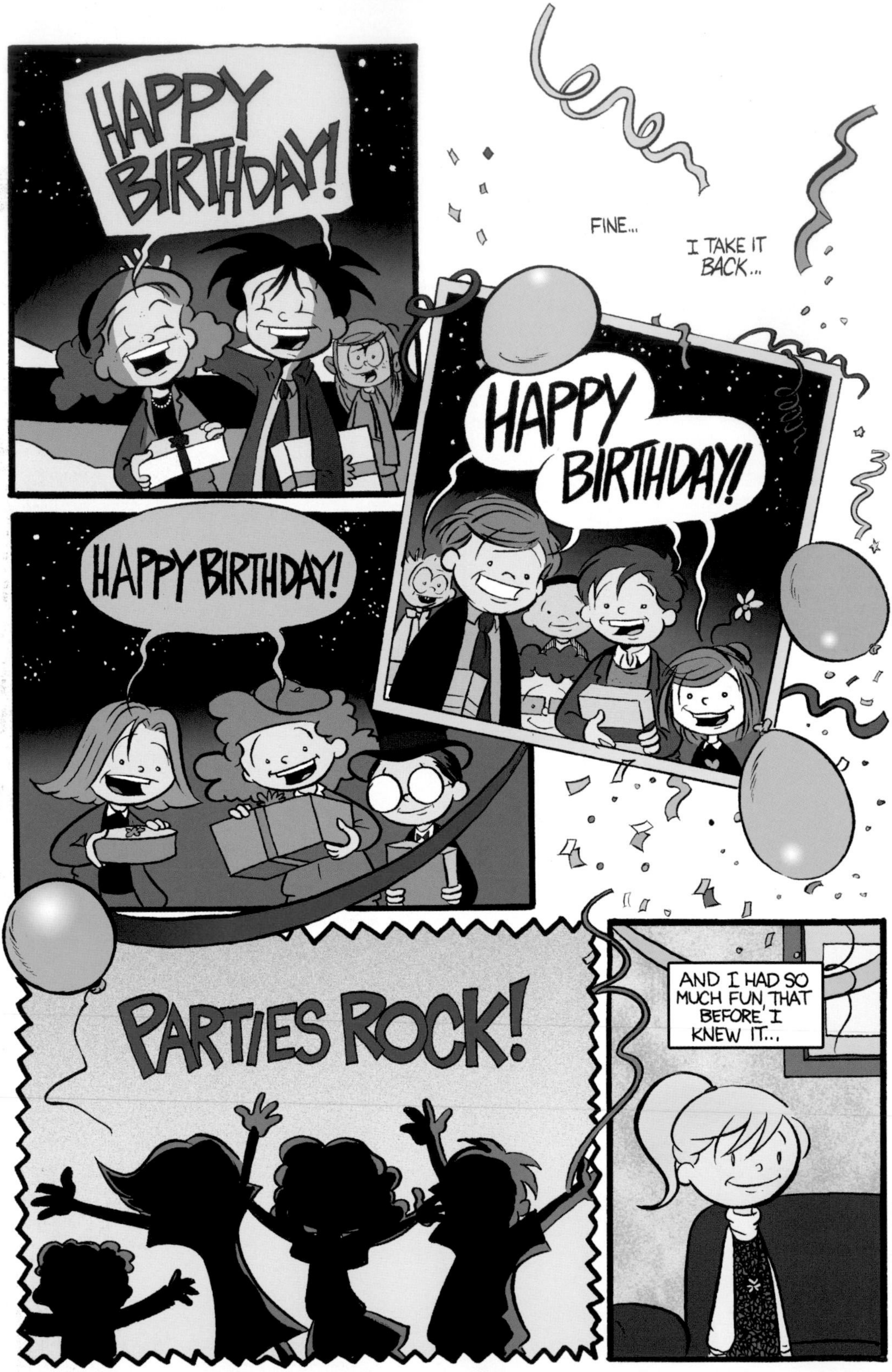
HAPPY BIRTHDAY!
FINE...
I TAKE IT BACK...
HAPPY BIRTHDAY!
HAPPY BIRTHDAY!
PARTIES ROCK!
AND I HAD SO MUCH FUN, THAT BEFORE I KNEW IT...

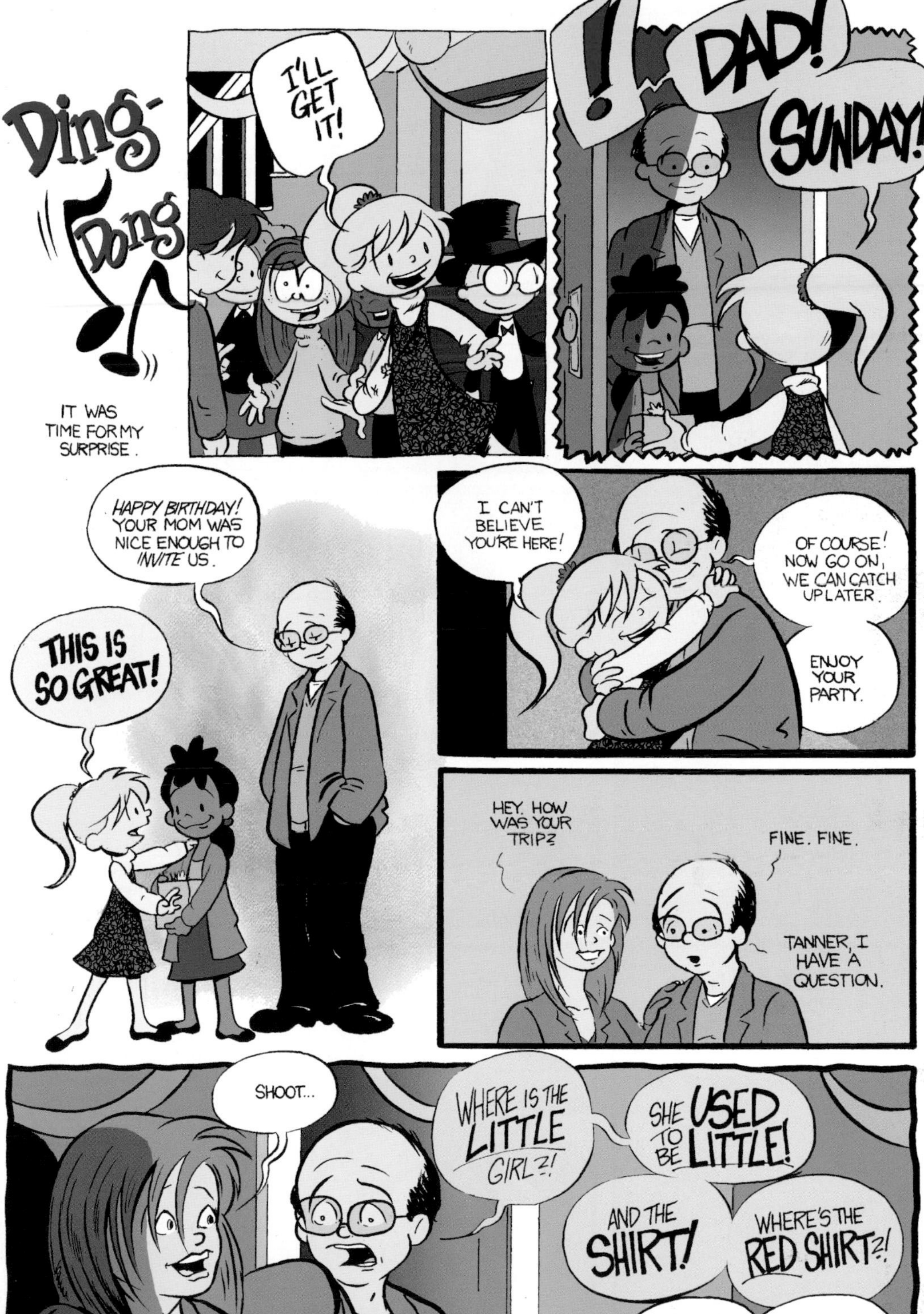
Ding-Dong
IT WAS TIME FOR MY SURPRISE.
I'LL GET IT!
!
DAD!
SUNDAY!
HAPPY BIRTHDAY! YOUR MOM WAS NICE ENOUGH TO INVITE US.
THIS IS SO GREAT!
I CAN'T BELIEVE YOU'RE HERE!
OF COURSE! NOW GO ON, WE CAN CATCH UP LATER.
ENJOY YOUR PARTY.
HEY. HOW WAS YOUR TRIP?
FINE. FINE.
TANNER, I HAVE A QUESTION.
SHOOT...
WHERE IS THE LITTLE GIRL?!
SHE USED TO BE LITTLE!
AND THE SHIRT!
WHERE'S THE RED SHIRT?!
HA HA HA HA HA
SHE'S STILL THAT KID....

SHE'S JUST WRAPPED IN A DIFFERENT PACKAGE.

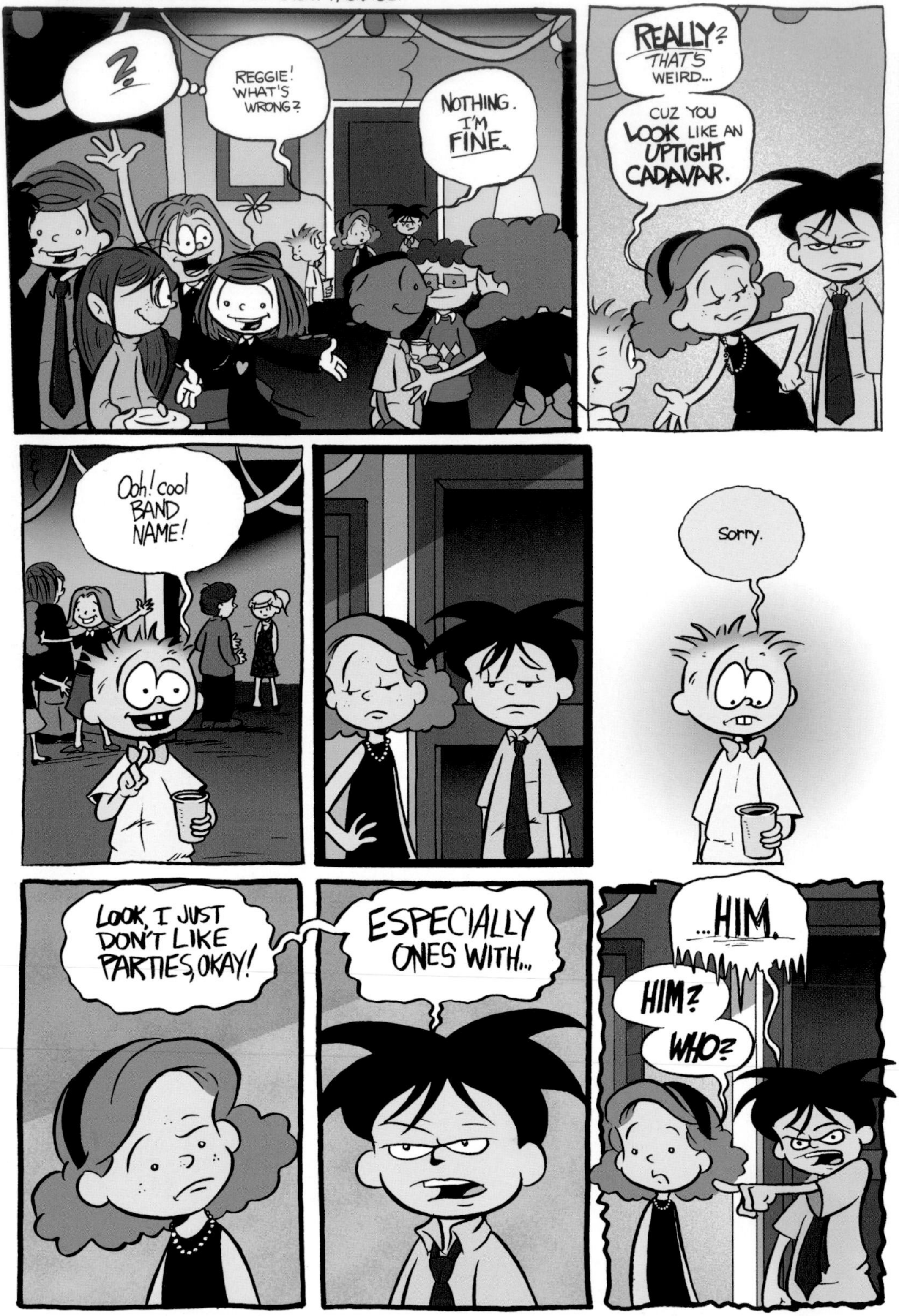
?
REGGIE! WHAT'S WRONG?
NOTHING. I'M FINE.
REALLY? THAT'S WEIRD...
CUZ YOU LOOK LIKE AN UPTIGHT CADAVAR.
Ooh! cool BAND NAME!
Sorry.
LOOK, I JUST DON'T LIKE PARTIES, OKAY!
ESPECIALLY ONES WITH...
...HIM.
HIM?
WHO?

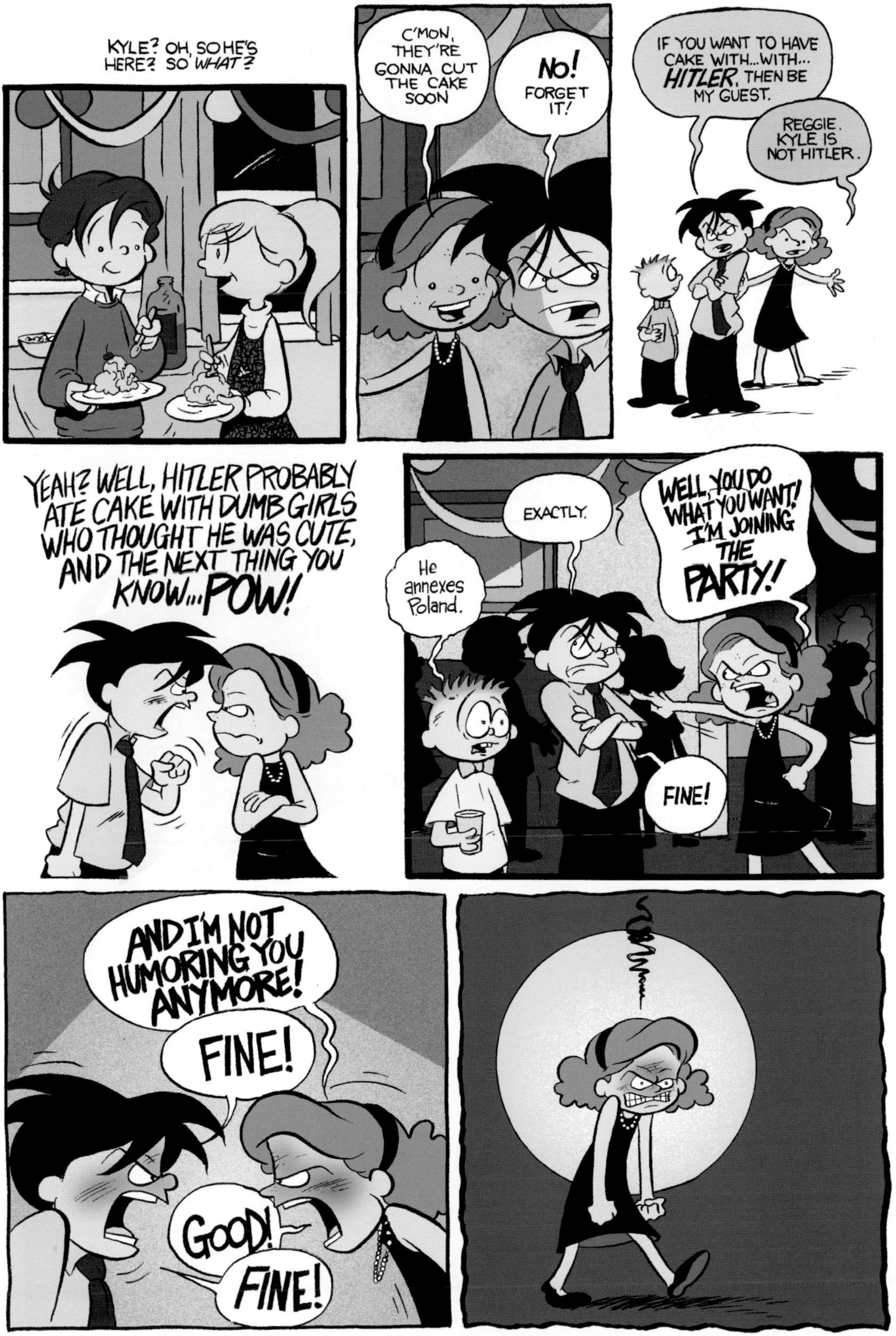
KYLE? OH, SO HE'S HERE? SO WHAT?
C'MON, THEY'RE GONNA CUT THE CAKE SOON
NO! FORGET IT!
IF YOU WANT TO HAVE CAKE WITH... WITH... HITLER, THEN BE MY GUEST.
REGGIE. KYLE IS NOT HITLER.
YEAH? WELL, HITLER PROBABLY ATE CAKE WITH DUMB GIRLS WHO THOUGHT HE WAS CUTE, AND THE NEXT THING YOU KNOW... POW!
He annexes Poland.
EXACTLY.
WELL, YOU DO WHAT YOU WANT! I'M JOINING THE PARTY!
FINE!
AND I'M NOT HUMORING YOU ANYMORE!
FINE!
GOOD!
FINE!

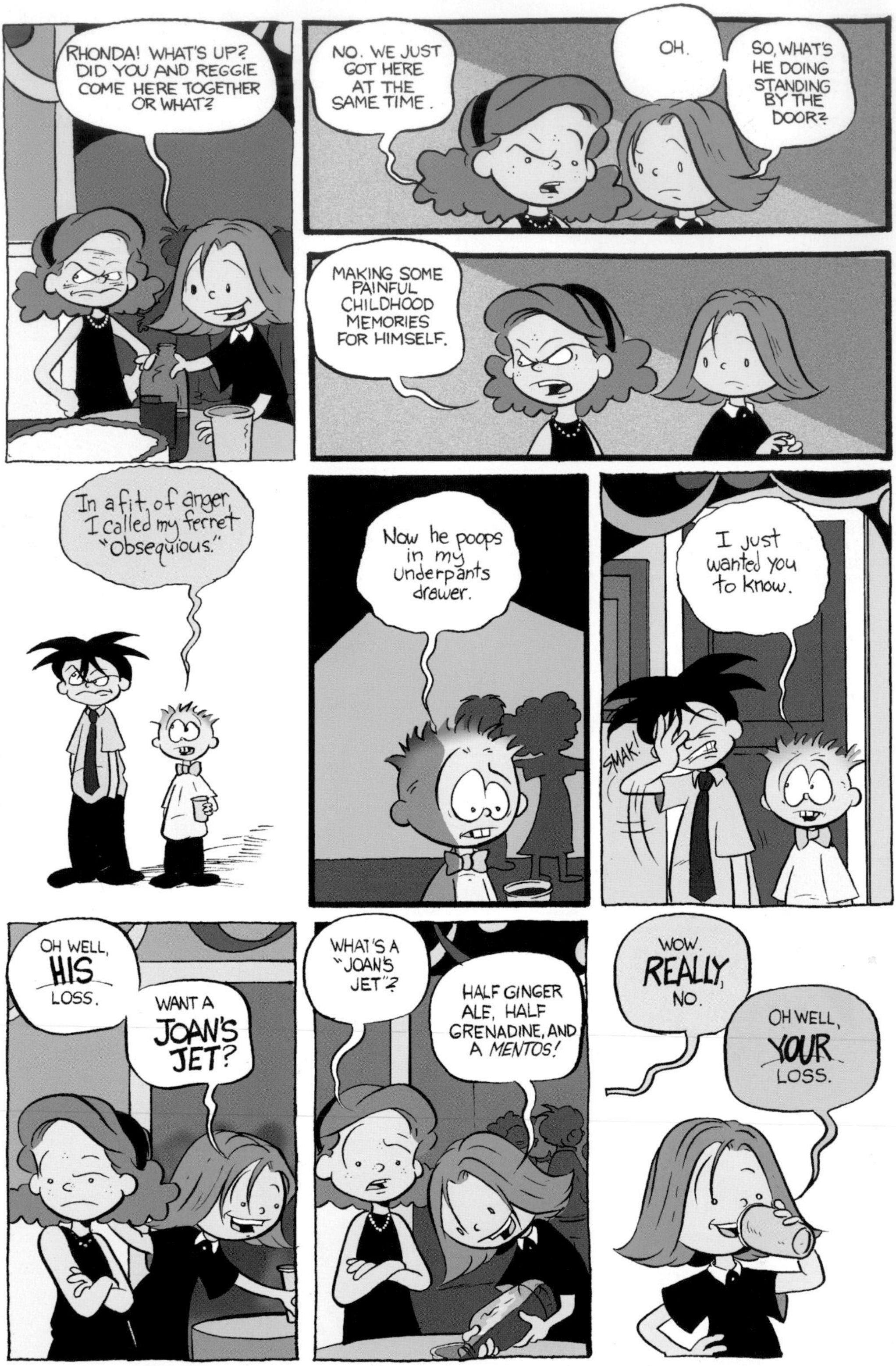
RHONDA! WHAT'S UP? DID YOU AND REGGIE COME HERE TOGETHER OR WHAT?
NO. WE JUST GOT HERE AT THE SAME TIME.
OH.
SO, WHAT'S HE DOING STANDING BY THE DOOR?
MAKING SOME PAINFUL CHILDHOOD MEMORIES FOR HIMSELF.
In a fit of anger, I called my ferret "obsequious."
Now he poops in my underpants drawer.
I just wanted you to know.
SMAK!
OH WELL, HIS LOSS.
WANT A JOAN'S JET?
WHAT'S A "JOAN'S JET"?
HALF GINGER ALE, HALF GRENADINE, AND A MENTOS!
WOW. REALLY, NO.
OH WELL, YOUR LOSS.

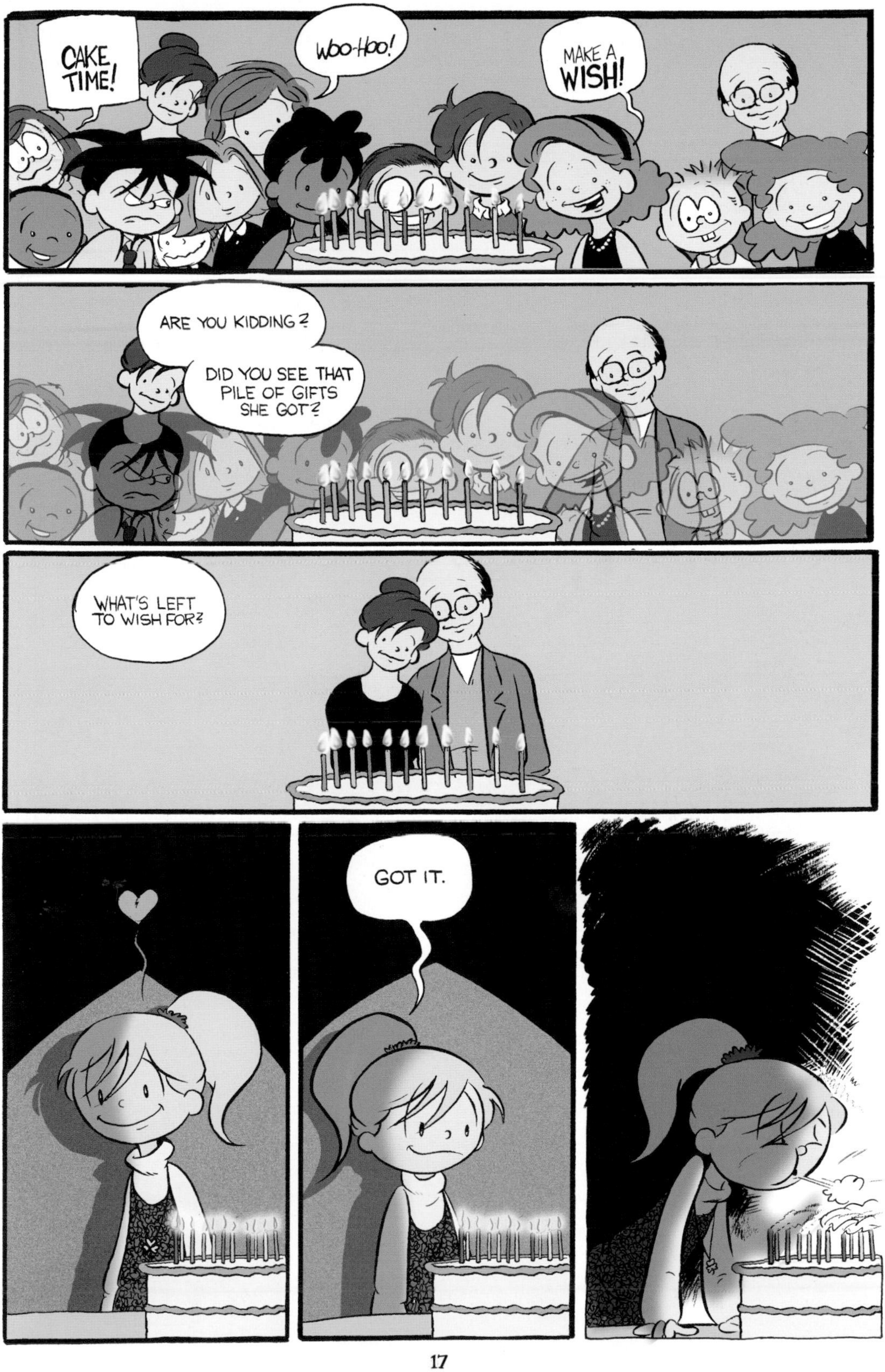
CAKE TIME!
WOO-HOO!
MAKE A WISH!
ARE YOU KIDDING?
DID YOU SEE THAT PILE OF GIFTS SHE GOT?
WHAT'S LEFT TO WISH FOR?
GOT IT.

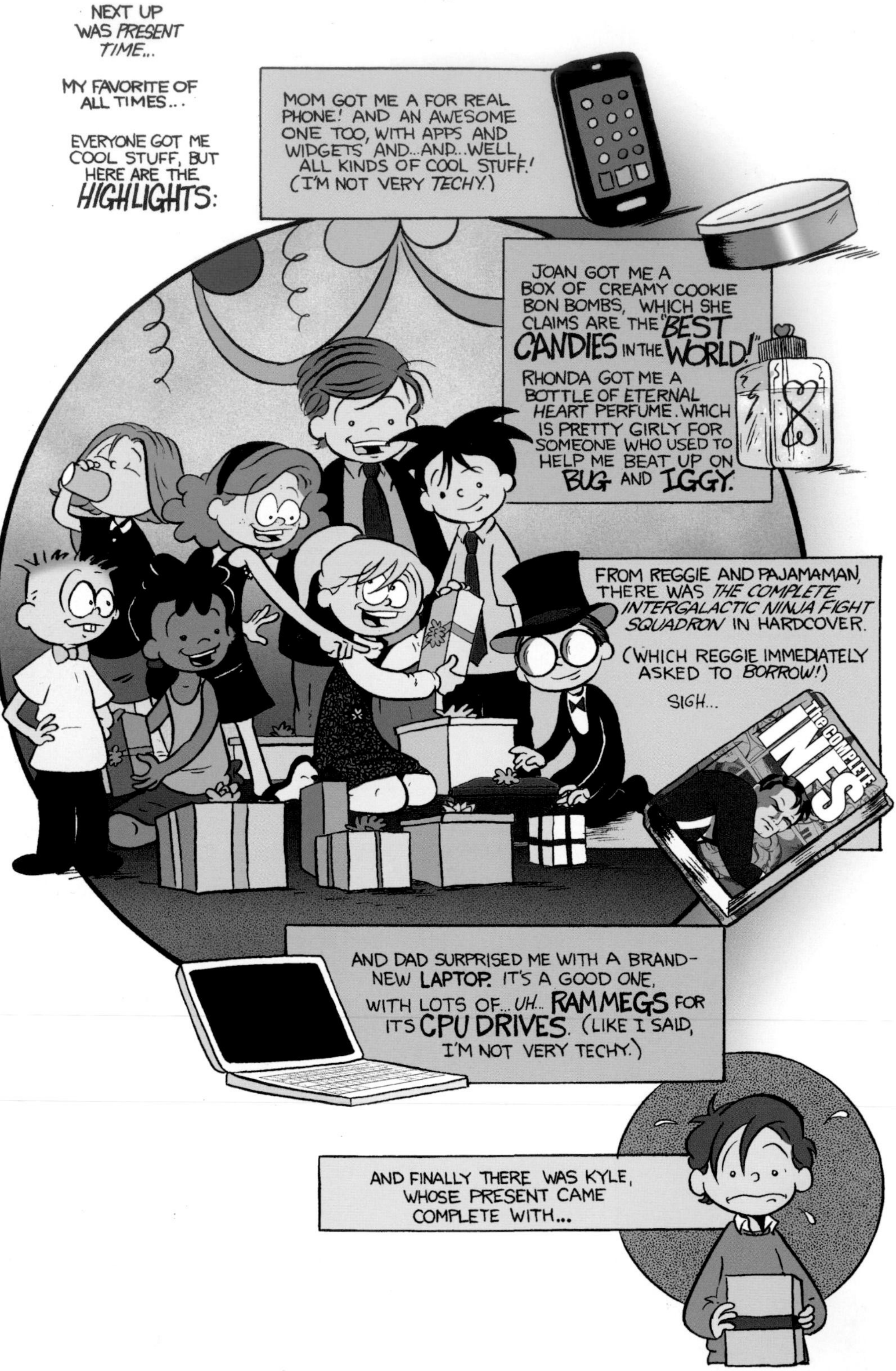
NEXT UP WAS PRESENT TIME...
MY FAVORITE OF ALL TIMES...
EVERYONE GOT ME COOL STUFF, BUT HERE ARE THE HIGHLIGHTS:
MOM GOT ME A FOR REAL PHONE! AND AN AWESOME ONE TOO, WITH APPS AND WIDGETS AND...AND...WELL, ALL KINDS OF COOL STUFF! (I'M NOT VERY TECHY.)
JOAN GOT ME A BOX OF CREAMY COOKIE BON BOMBS, WHICH SHE CLAIMS ARE THE "BEST CANDIES IN THE WORLD!"
RHONDA GOT ME A BOTTLE OF ETERNAL HEART PERFUME. WHICH IS PRETTY GIRLY FOR SOMEONE WHO USED TO HELP ME BEAT UP ON BUG AND IGGY.
FROM REGGIE AND PAJAMAMAN, THERE WAS THE COMPLETE INTERGALACTIC NINJA FIGHT SQUADRON IN HARDCOVER.
(WHICH REGGIE IMMEDIATELY ASKED TO BORROW!)
SIGH...
The COMPLETE INFS
AND DAD SURPRISED ME WITH A BRAND-NEW LAPTOP. IT'S A GOOD ONE, WITH LOTS OF... UH... RAM MEGS FOR ITS CPU DRIVES. (LIKE I SAID, I'M NOT VERY TECHY.)
AND FINALLY THERE WAS KYLE, WHOSE PRESENT CAME COMPLETE WITH...

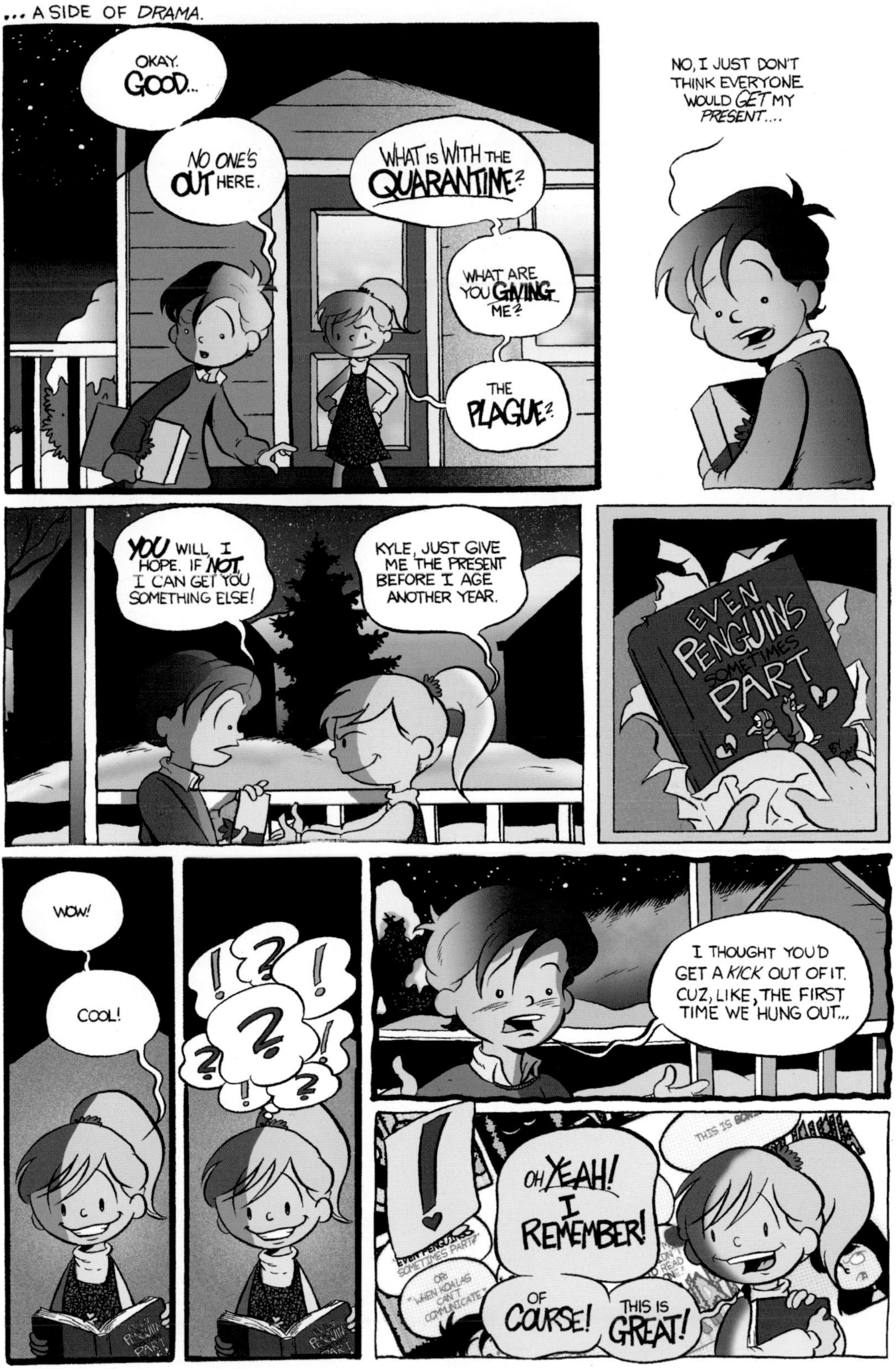
... A SIDE OF DRAMA.
OKAY. GOOD...
NO ONE'S OUT HERE.
WHAT IS WITH THE QUARANTINE?
WHAT ARE YOU GIVING ME?
THE PLAGUE?
NO, I JUST DON'T THINK EVERYONE WOULD GET MY PRESENT....
YOU WILL, I HOPE. IF NOT, I CAN GET YOU SOMETHING ELSE!
KYLE, JUST GIVE ME THE PRESENT BEFORE I AGE ANOTHER YEAR.
EVEN PENGUINS SOMETIMES PART
WOW!
COOL!
I THOUGHT YOU'D GET A KICK OUT OF IT. CUZ, LIKE, THE FIRST TIME WE HUNG OUT...
"EVEN PENGUINS SOMETIMES PART?"
OR: "WHEN KOALAS CAN'T COMMUNICATE"
OH YEAH! I REMEMBER!
OF COURSE!
THIS IS GREAT!

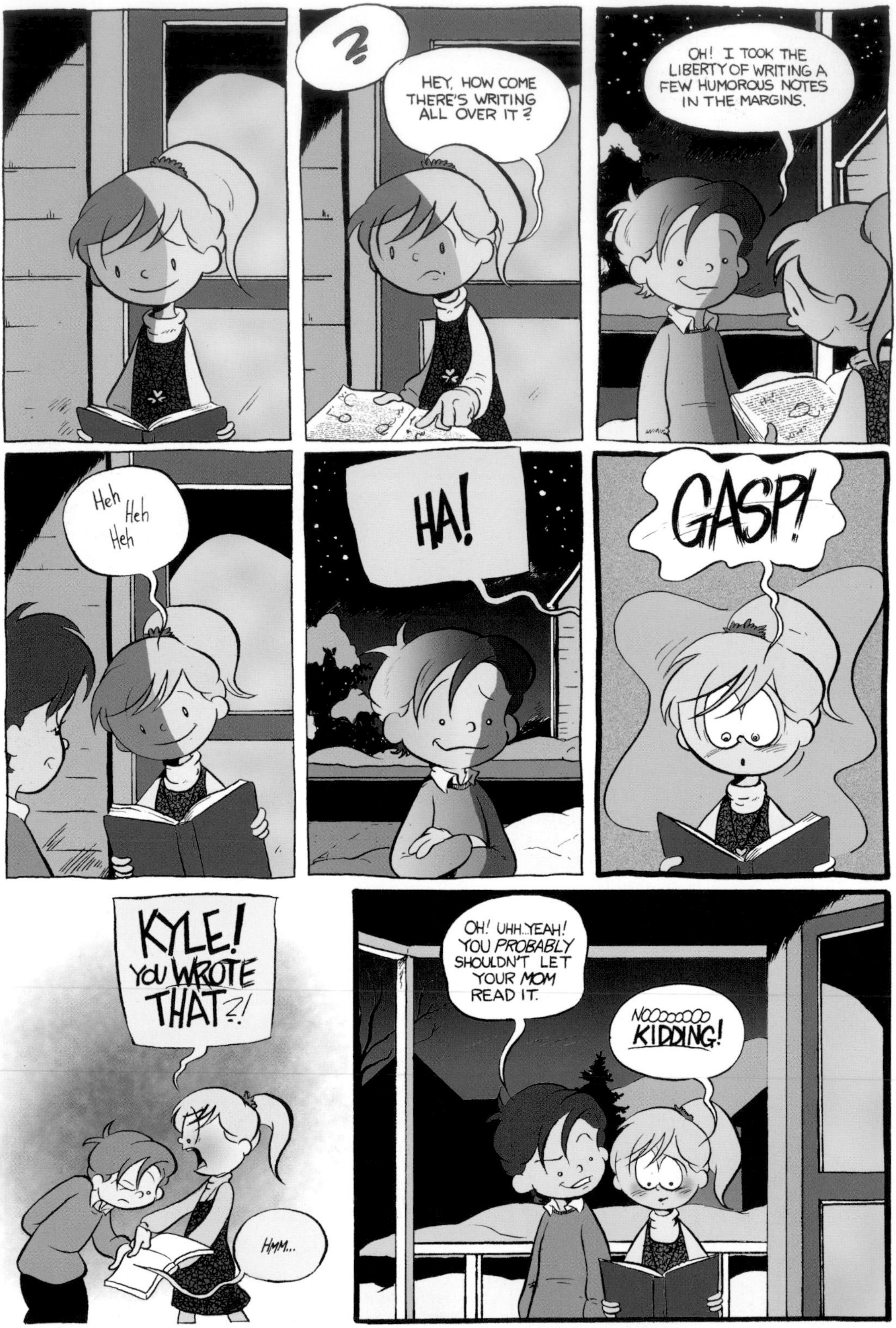
?
HEY, HOW COME THERE'S WRITING ALL OVER IT?
OH! I TOOK THE LIBERTY OF WRITING A FEW HUMOROUS NOTES IN THE MARGINS.
Heh Heh Heh
HA!
GASP!
KYLE! YOU WROTE THAT?!
HMM...
OH! UHH...YEAH! YOU PROBABLY SHOULDN'T LET YOUR MOM READ IT.
NOOoooooo KIDDING!

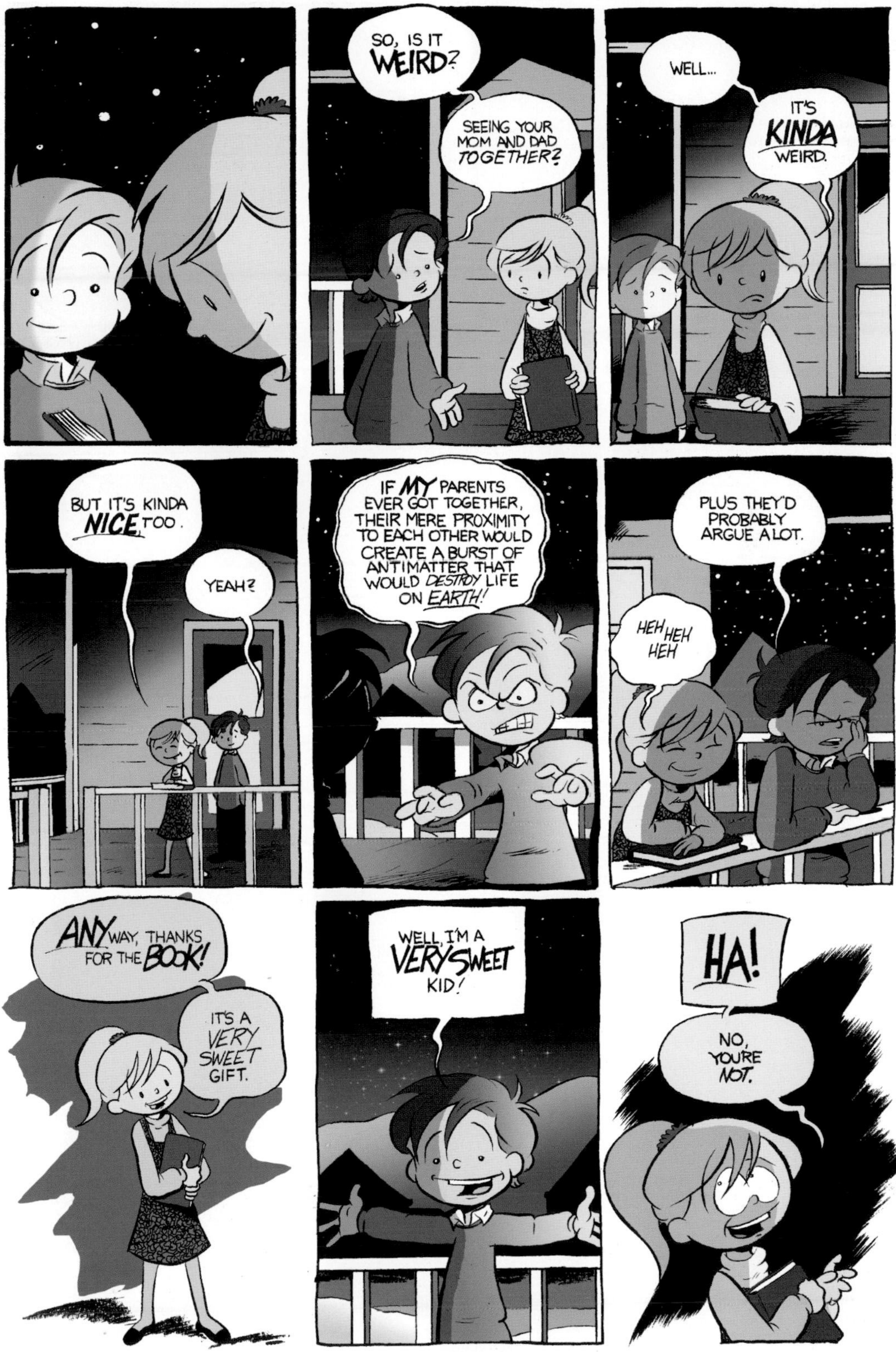
SO, IS IT WEIRD?
SEEING YOUR MOM AND DAD TOGETHER?
WELL...
IT'S KINDA WEIRD.
BUT IT'S KINDA NICE, TOO.
YEAH?
IF MY PARENTS EVER GOT TOGETHER, THEIR MERE PROXIMITY TO EACH OTHER WOULD CREATE A BURST OF ANTIMATTER THAT WOULD DESTROY LIFE ON EARTH!
PLUS THEY'D PROBABLY ARGUE A LOT.
HEH HEH HEH
ANYWAY, THANKS FOR THE BOOK!
IT'S A VERY SWEET GIFT.
WELL, I'M A VERY SWEET KID!
HA!
NO, YOU'RE NOT.

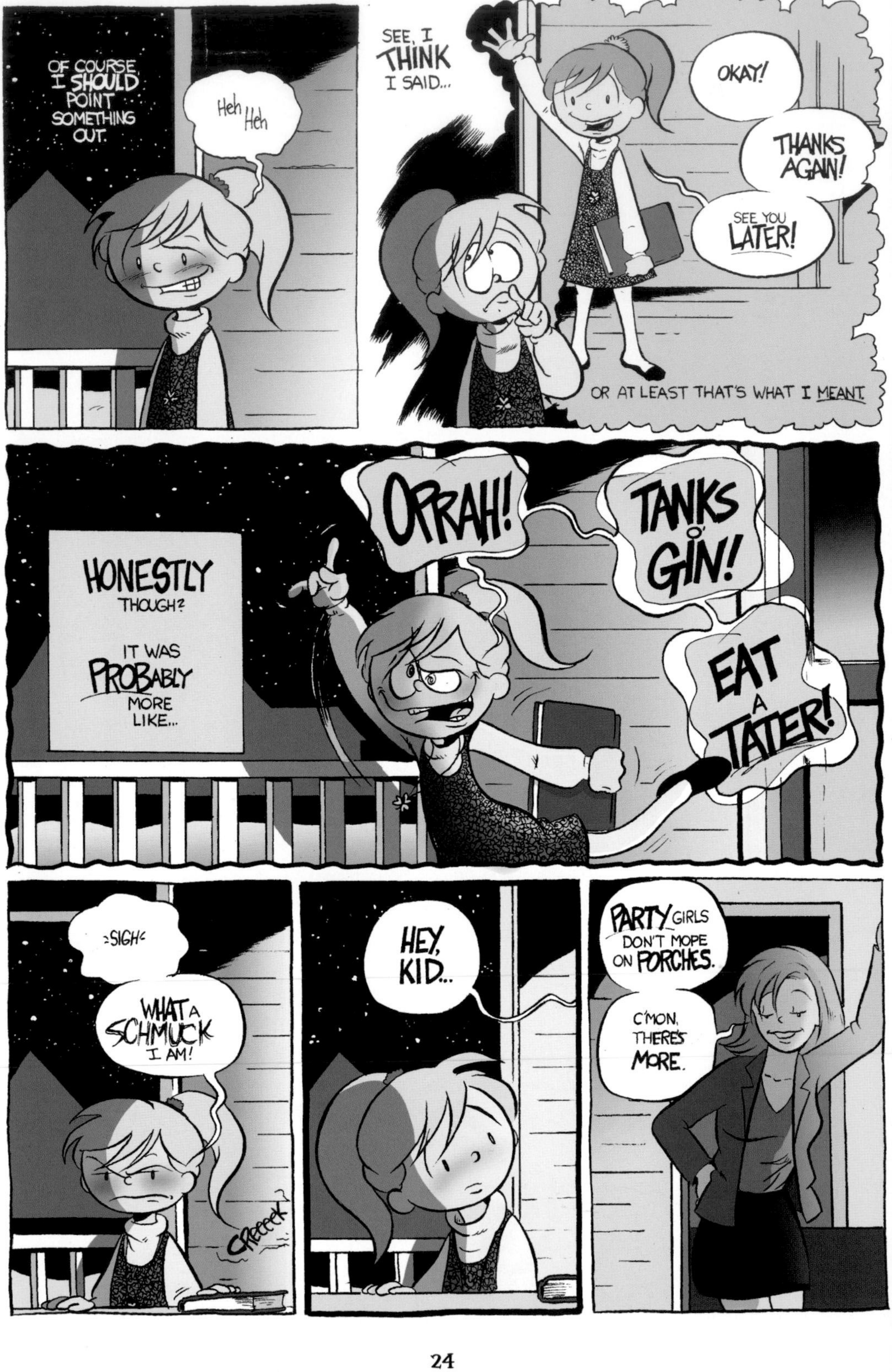

OF COURSE, I SHOULD POINT SOMETHING OUT.
Heh Heh
SEE, I THINK I SAID...
OKAY!
THANKS AGAIN!
SEE YOU LATER!
OR AT LEAST THAT'S WHAT I MEANT.
HONESTLY THOUGH? IT WAS PROBABLY MORE LIKE...
OPRAH!
TANKS O' GIN!
EAT A TATER!
SIGH
WHAT A SCHMUCK I AM!
CREEEEK
HEY, KID...
PARTY GIRLS DON'T MOPE ON PORCHES.
C'MON, THERE'S MORE.

25

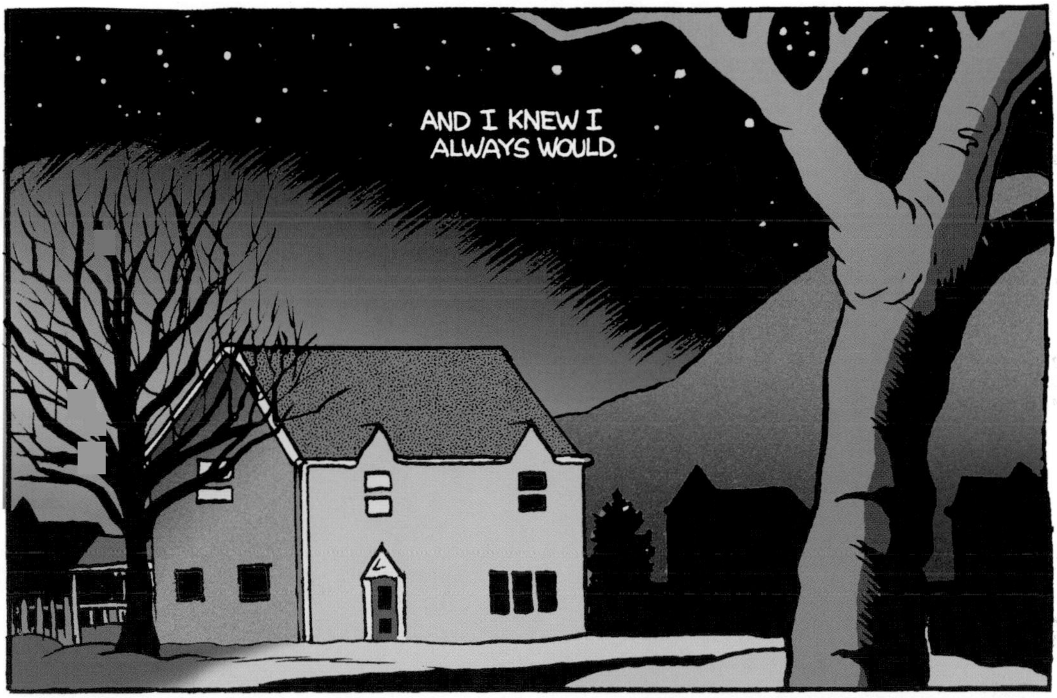
AND I KNEW I ALWAYS WOULD.

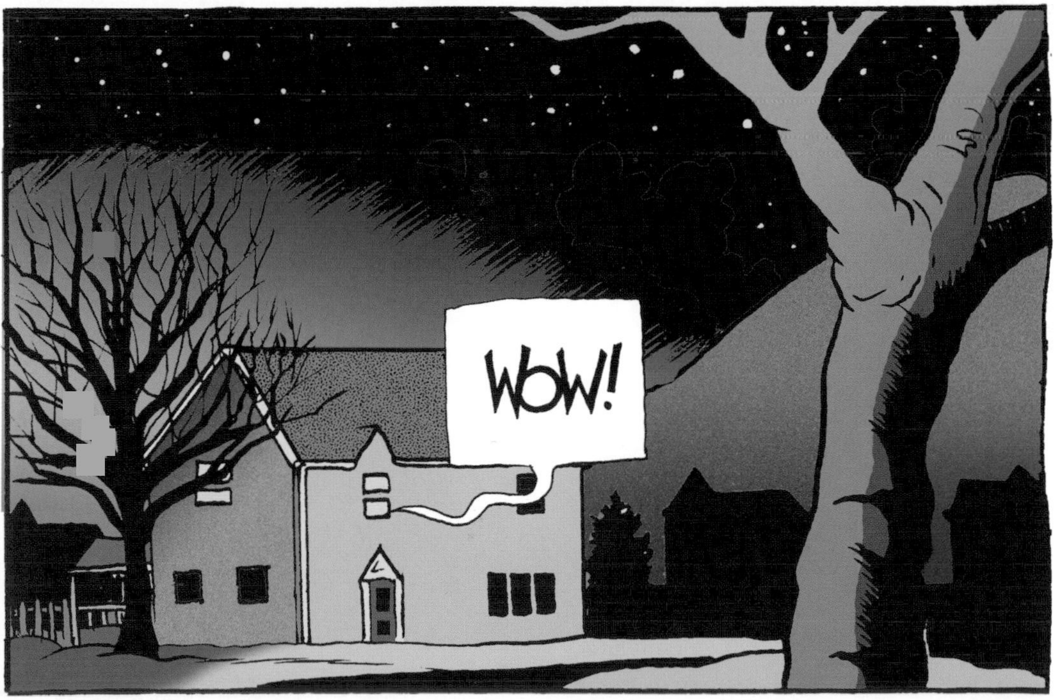
WOW!

29

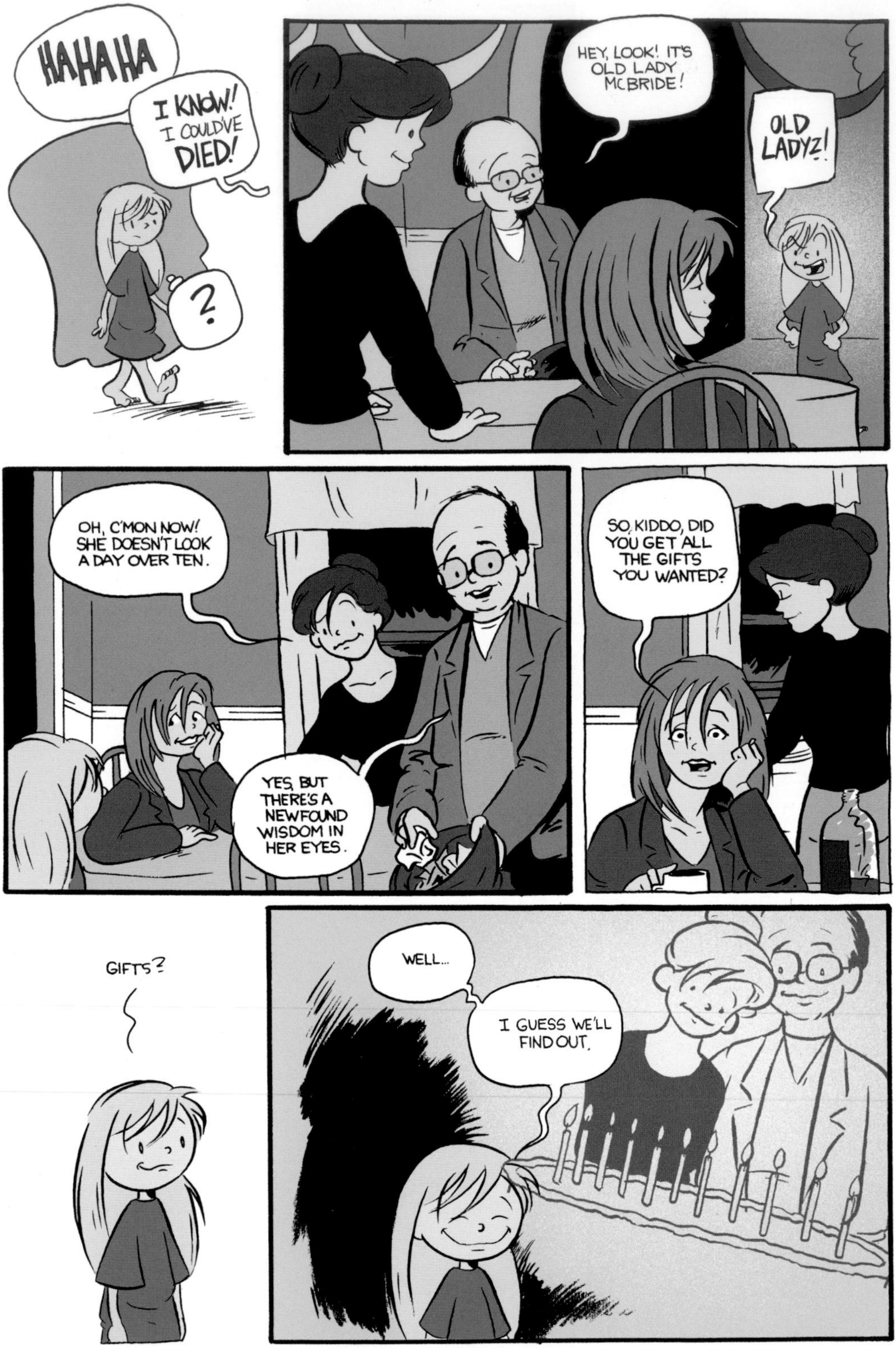
HAHAHA
I KNOW! I COULD'VE DIED!
?
HEY, LOOK! IT'S OLD LADY MCBRIDE!
OLD LADYZ!
OH, C'MON NOW! SHE DOESN'T LOOK A DAY OVER TEN.
YES, BUT THERE'S A NEWFOUND WISDOM IN HER EYES.
SO, KIDDO, DID YOU GET ALL THE GIFTS YOU WANTED?
GIFTS?
WELL...
I GUESS WE'LL FIND OUT.

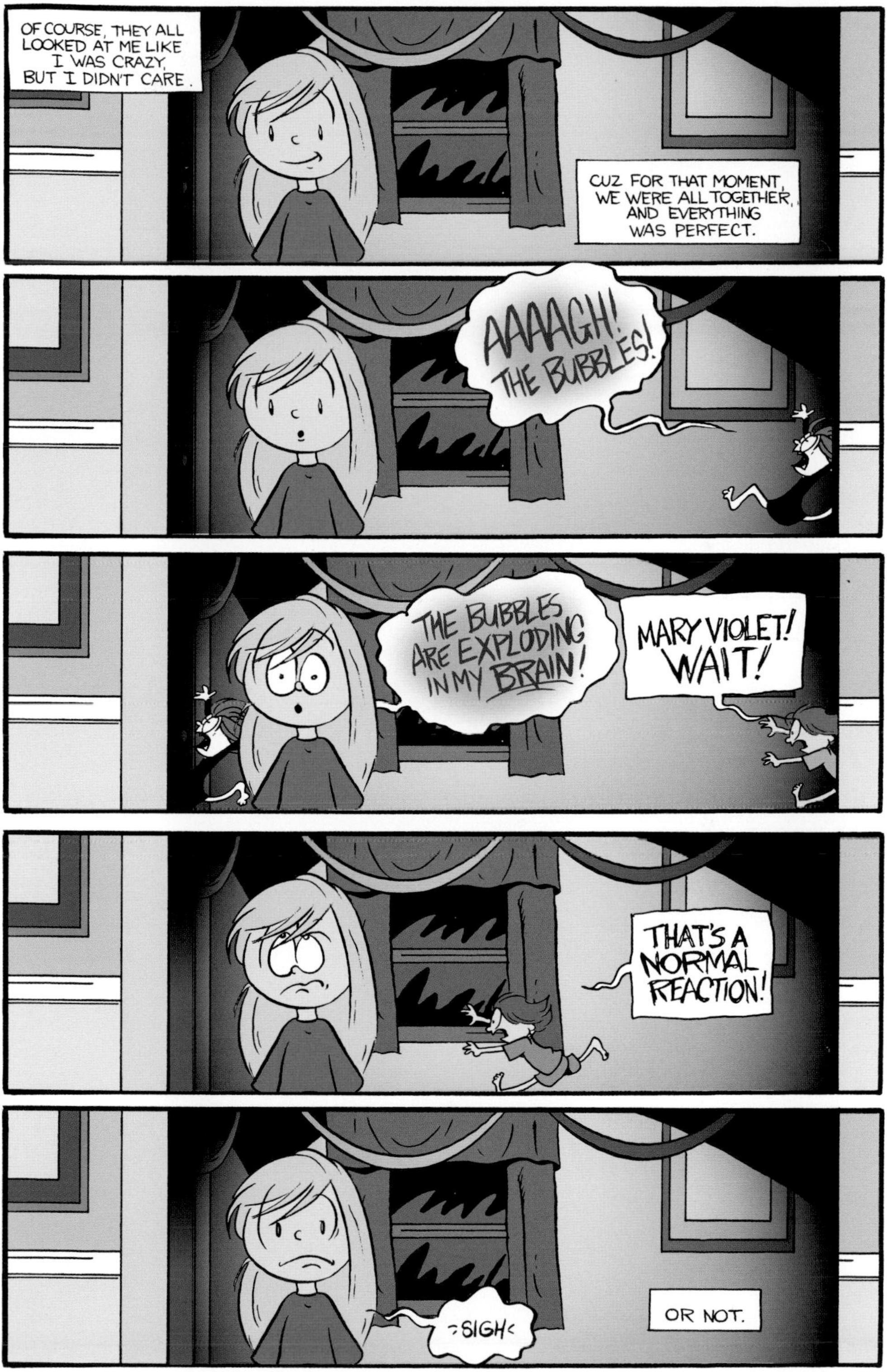
OF COURSE, THEY ALL LOOKED AT ME LIKE I WAS CRAZY, BUT I DIDN'T CARE.
CUZ FOR THAT MOMENT, WE WERE ALL TOGETHER, AND EVERYTHING WAS PERFECT.
AAAAGH! THE BUBBLES!
THE BUBBLES ARE EXPLODING IN MY BRAIN!
MARY VIOLET! WAIT!
THAT'S A NORMAL REACTION!
>SIGH<
OR NOT.

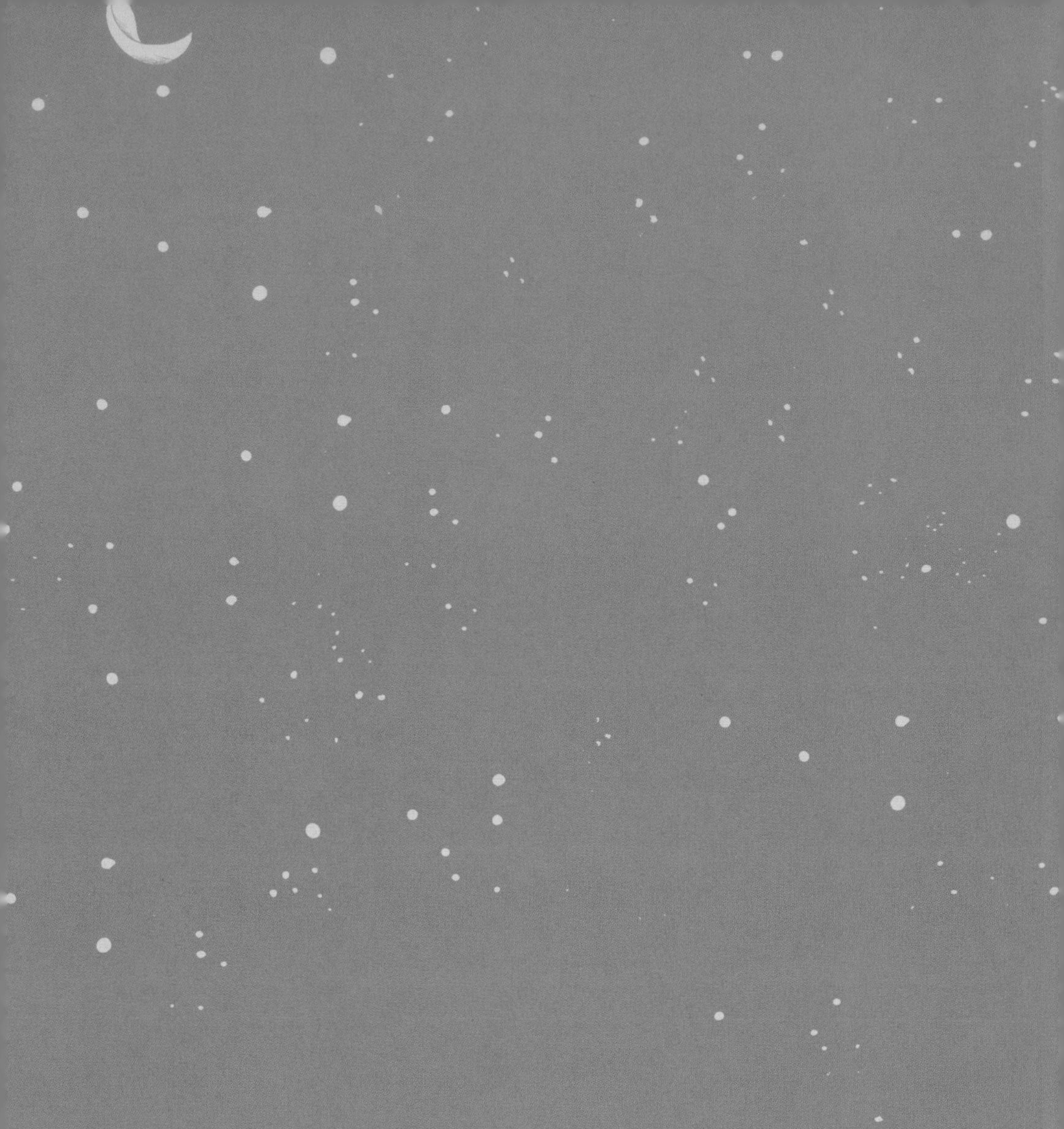

"I'm still waiting to use algebra."

–Tanner Clark

from a profile printed in her high school alumni newsletter

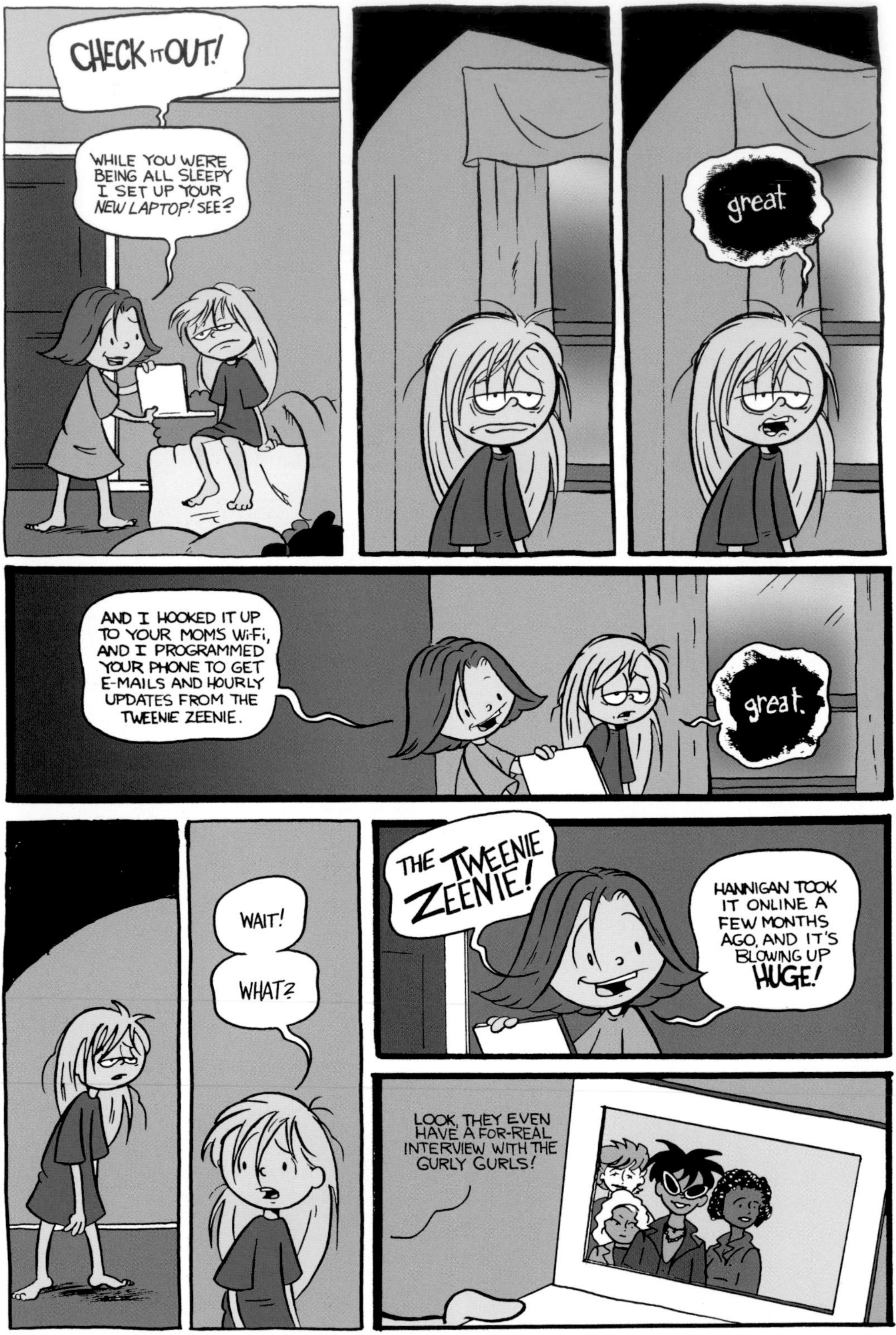
CHECK IT OUT!
WHILE YOU WERE BEING ALL SLEEPY I SET UP YOUR NEW LAPTOP! SEE?
great.
AND I HOOKED IT UP TO YOUR MOM'S Wi-Fi, AND I PROGRAMMED YOUR PHONE TO GET E-MAILS AND HOURLY UPDATES FROM THE TWEENIE ZEENIE.
great.
WAIT!
WHAT?
THE TWEENIE ZEENIE!
HANNIGAN TOOK IT ONLINE A FEW MONTHS AGO, AND IT'S BLOWING UP HUGE!
LOOK, THEY EVEN HAVE A FOR-REAL INTERVIEW WITH THE GURLY GURLS!

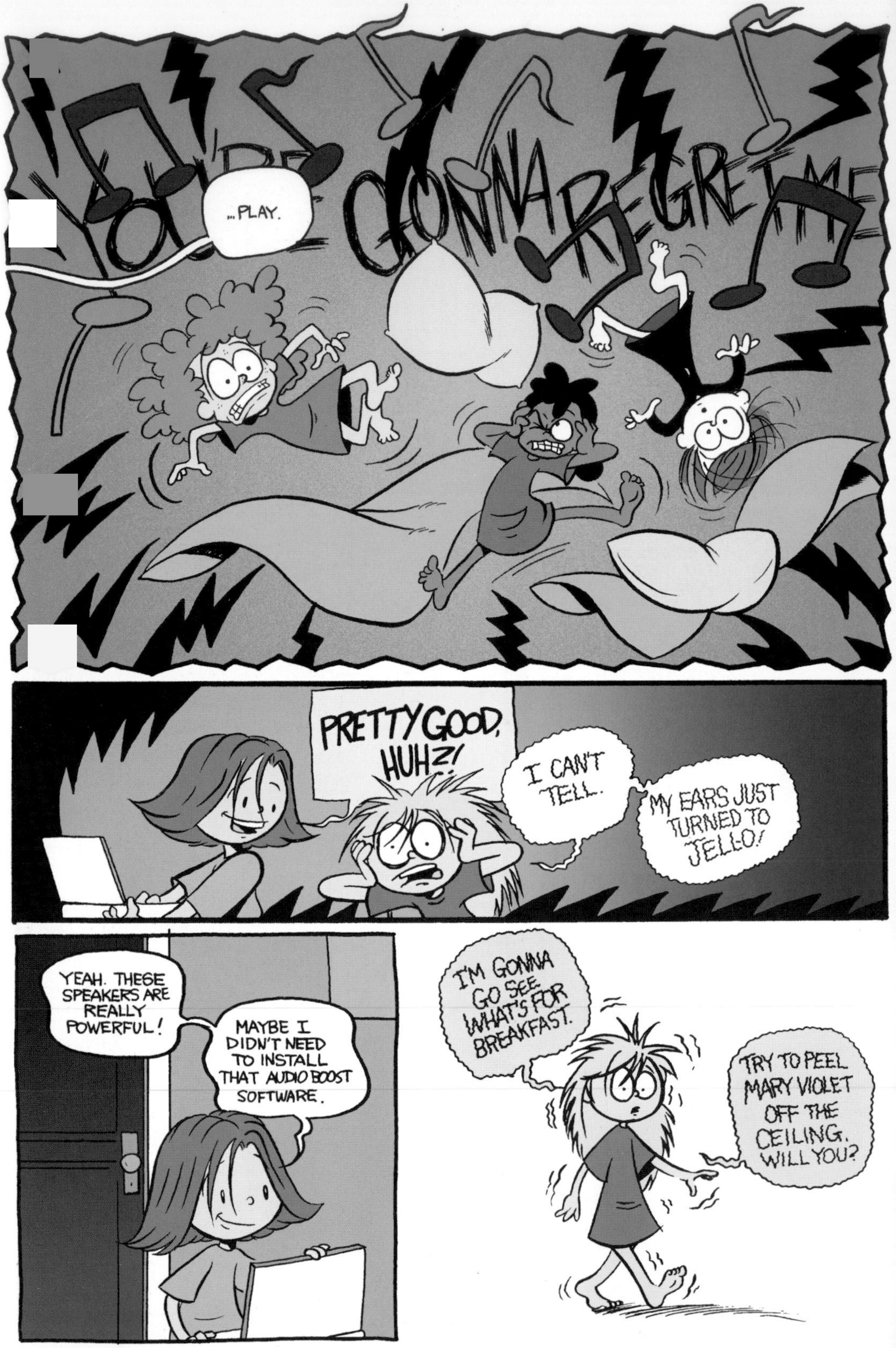
...PLAY.
GONNA REGRET ME
PRETTY GOOD, HUH?!
I CAN'T TELL.
MY EARS JUST TURNED TO JELL-O!
YEAH. THESE SPEAKERS ARE REALLY POWERFUL!
MAYBE I DIDN'T NEED TO INSTALL THAT AUDIO BOOST SOFTWARE.
I'M GONNA GO SEE WHAT'S FOR BREAKFAST.
TRY TO PEEL MARY VIOLET OFF THE CEILING, WILL YOU?

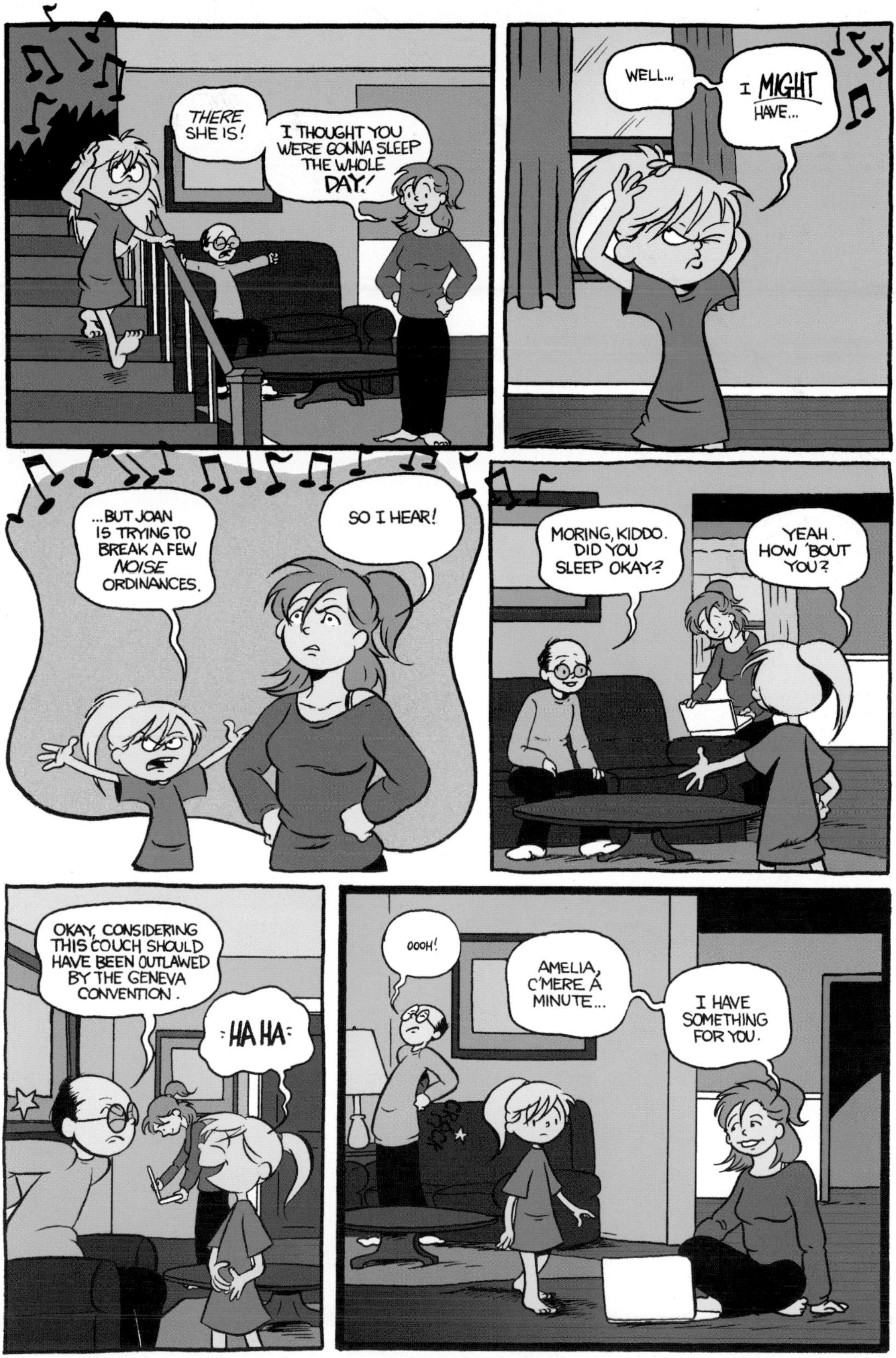
THERE SHE IS!
I THOUGHT YOU WERE GONNA SLEEP THE WHOLE DAY!
WELL...
I MIGHT HAVE...
...BUT JOAN IS TRYING TO BREAK A FEW NOISE ORDINANCES.
SO I HEAR!
MORING, KIDDO. DID YOU SLEEP OKAY?
YEAH. HOW 'BOUT YOU?
OKAY, CONSIDERING THIS COUCH SHOULD HAVE BEEN OUTLAWED BY THE GENEVA CONVENTION.
HA HA
OOOH!
AMELIA, C'MERE A MINUTE...
I HAVE SOMETHING FOR YOU.

40

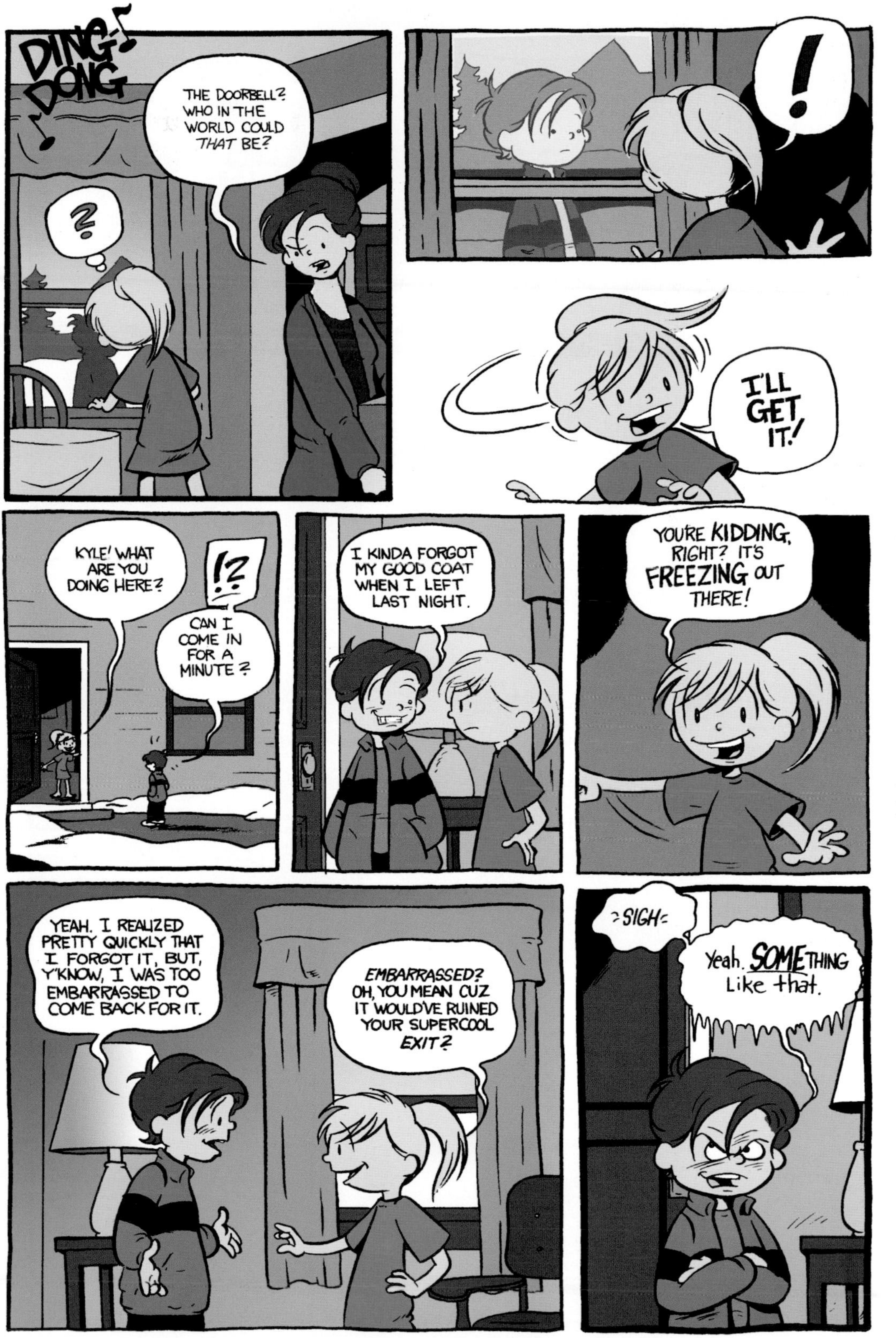
DING-DONG
THE DOORBELL? WHO IN THE WORLD COULD THAT BE?
?
!
I'LL GET IT!
KYLE! WHAT ARE YOU DOING HERE?
!?
CAN I COME IN FOR A MINUTE?
I KINDA FORGOT MY GOOD COAT WHEN I LEFT LAST NIGHT.
YOU'RE KIDDING, RIGHT? IT'S FREEZING OUT THERE!
YEAH. I REALIZED PRETTY QUICKLY THAT I FORGOT IT, BUT, Y'KNOW, I WAS TOO EMBARRASSED TO COME BACK FOR IT.
EMBARRASSED? OH, YOU MEAN CUZ IT WOULD'VE RUINED YOUR SUPERCOOL EXIT?
SIGH
Yeah. SOMETHING Like that.

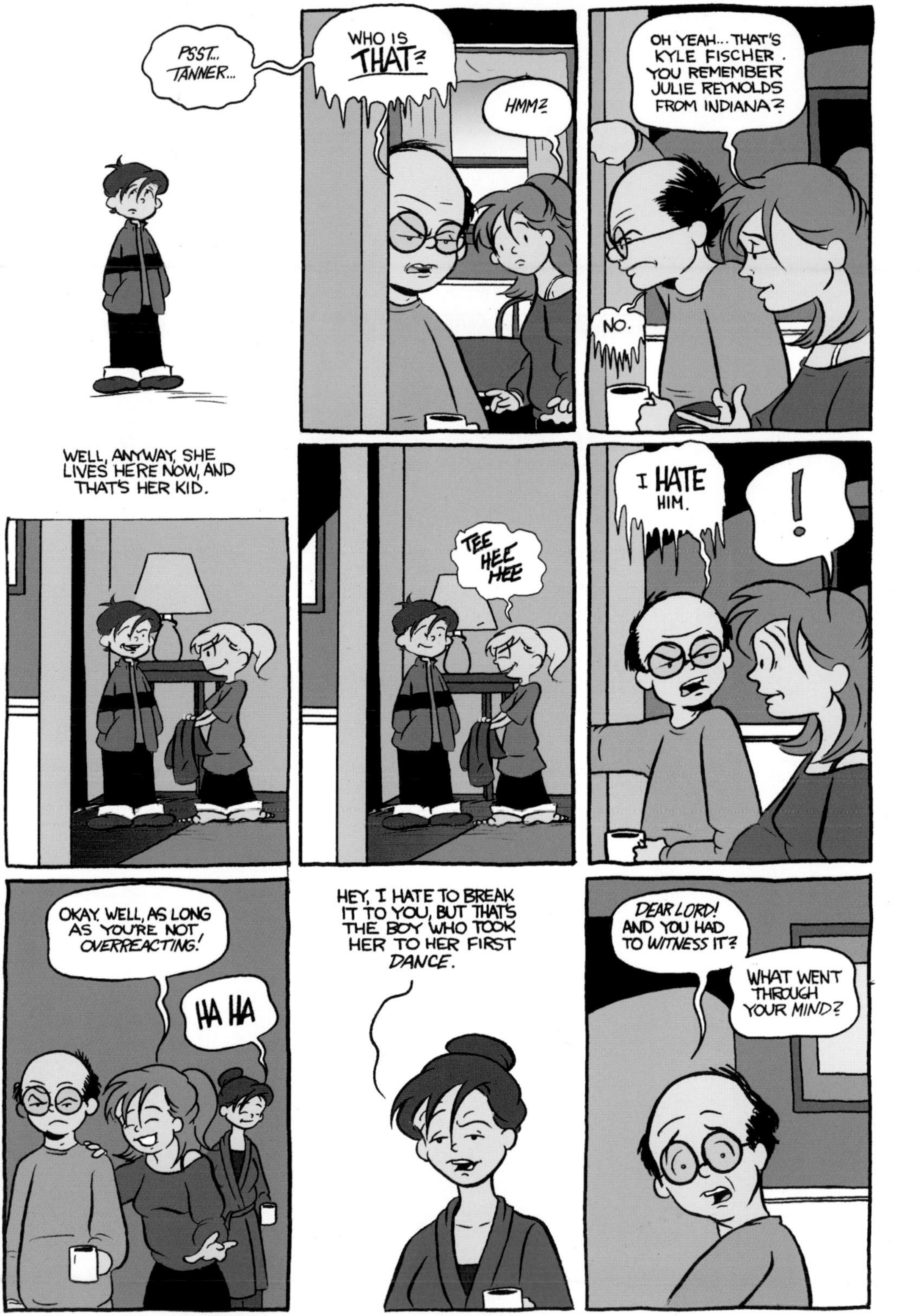
PSST... TANNER...
WHO IS THAT?
HMM?
OH YEAH... THAT'S KYLE FISCHER. YOU REMEMBER JULIE REYNOLDS FROM INDIANA?
NO.
WELL, ANYWAY, SHE LIVES HERE NOW, AND THAT'S HER KID.
TEE HEE HEE
I HATE HIM.
!
OKAY. WELL, AS LONG AS YOU'RE NOT OVERREACTING!
HA HA
HEY, I HATE TO BREAK IT TO YOU, BUT THAT'S THE BOY WHO TOOK HER TO HER FIRST DANCE.
DEAR LORD! AND YOU HAD TO WITNESS IT?
WHAT WENT THROUGH YOUR MIND?

44

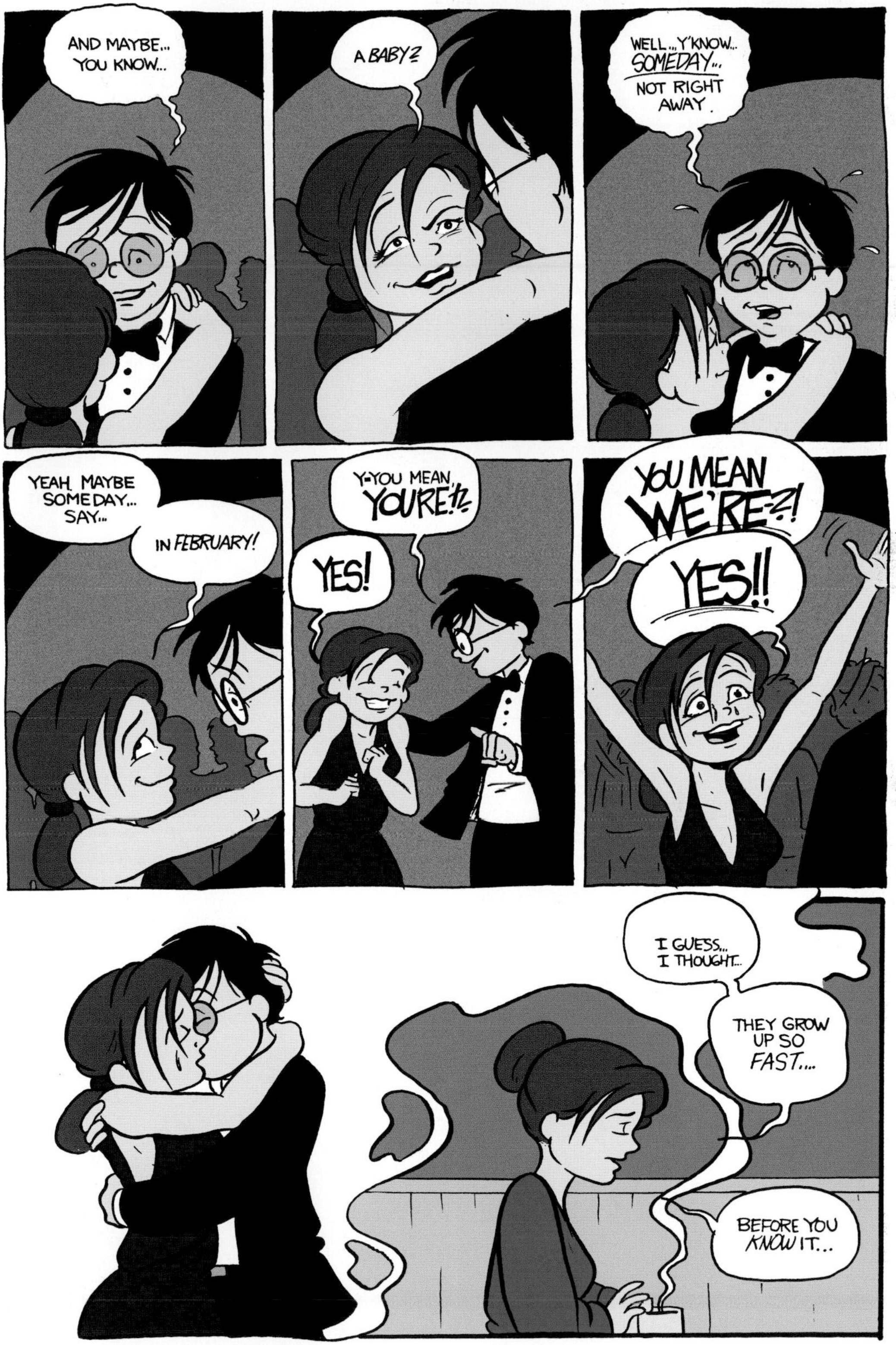
AND MAYBE... YOU KNOW...
A BABY?!
WELL... Y'KNOW... SOMEDAY... NOT RIGHT AWAY.
YEAH. MAYBE SOMEDAY... SAY...
IN FEBRUARY!
Y-YOU MEAN, YOU'RE?!
YES!
YOU MEAN WE'RE?!
YES!!
I GUESS... I THOUGHT...
THEY GROW UP SO FAST....
BEFORE YOU KNOW IT...

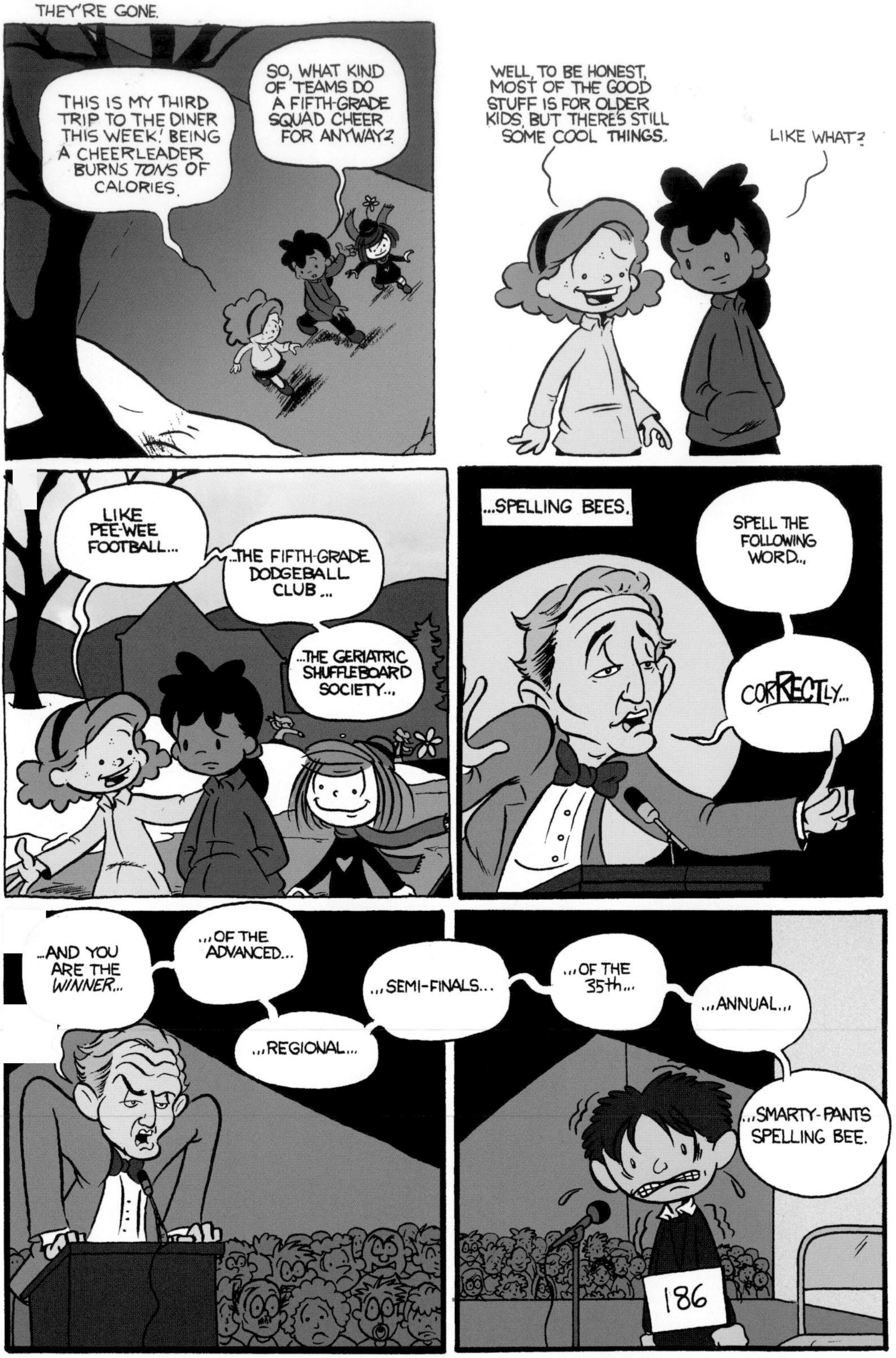
THEY'RE GONE.
THIS IS MY THIRD TRIP TO THE DINER THIS WEEK! BEING A CHEERLEADER BURNS TONS OF CALORIES.
SO, WHAT KIND OF TEAMS DO A FIFTH-GRADE SQUAD CHEER FOR ANYWAY?
WELL, TO BE HONEST, MOST OF THE GOOD STUFF IS FOR OLDER KIDS, BUT THERE'S STILL SOME COOL THINGS.
LIKE WHAT?
LIKE PEE-WEE FOOTBALL...
...THE FIFTH-GRADE DODGEBALL CLUB...
...THE GERIATRIC SHUFFLEBOARD SOCIETY...
...SPELLING BEES.
SPELL THE FOLLOWING WORD...
CORRECTLY...
...AND YOU ARE THE WINNER...
...OF THE ADVANCED...
...REGIONAL...
...SEMI-FINALS...
...OF THE 35th...
...ANNUAL...
...SMARTY-PANTS SPELLING BEE.
186

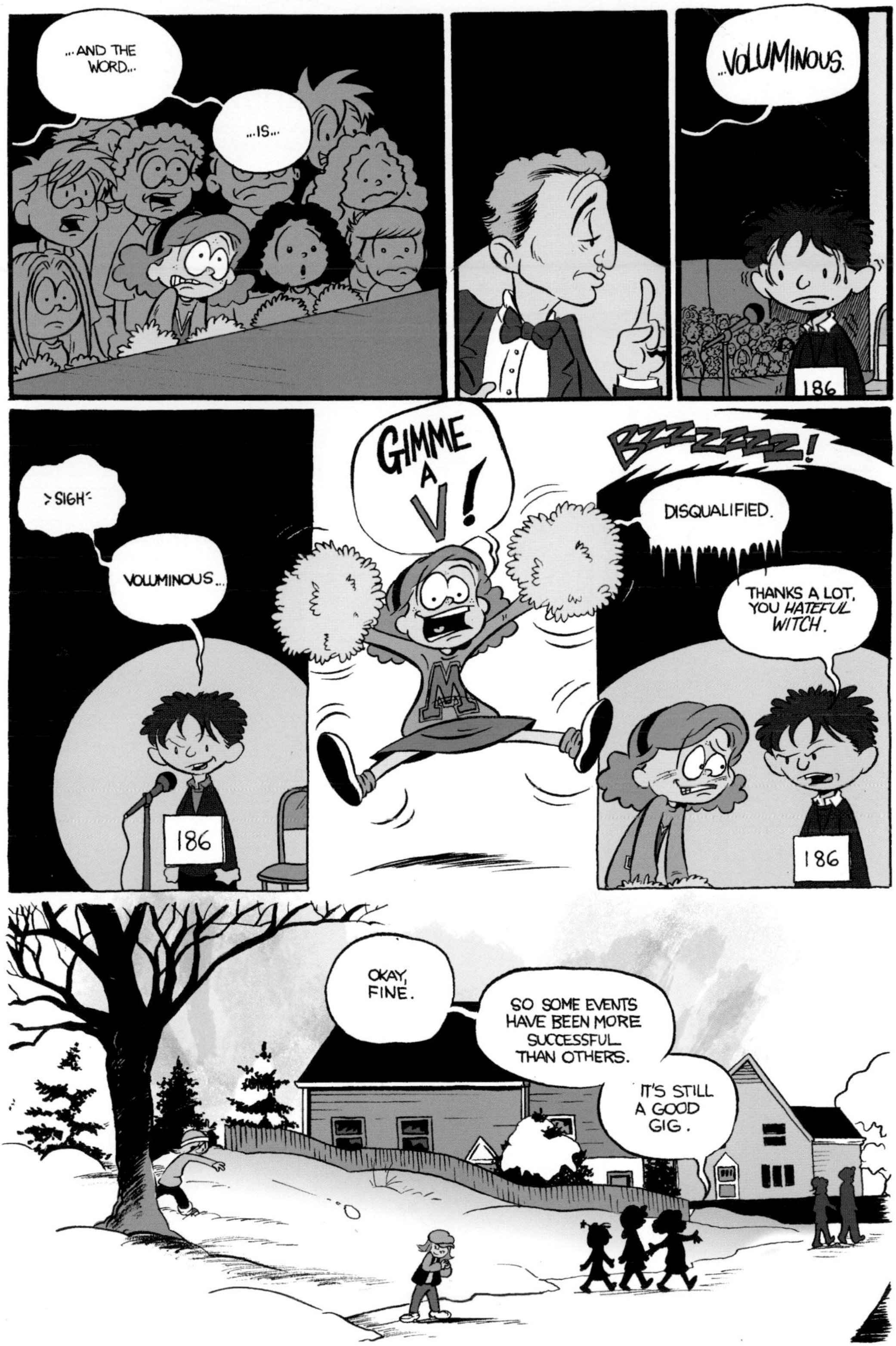
...AND THE WORD...
...IS...
...VOLUMINOUS.
186
>SIGH<
VOLUMINOUS...
186
GIMME A V!
M
BZZZZZZZ!
DISQUALIFIED.
THANKS A LOT, YOU *HATEFUL* *WITCH*.
186
OKAY, FINE.
SO SOME EVENTS HAVE BEEN MORE SUCCESSFUL THAN OTHERS.
IT'S STILL A GOOD GIG.

48

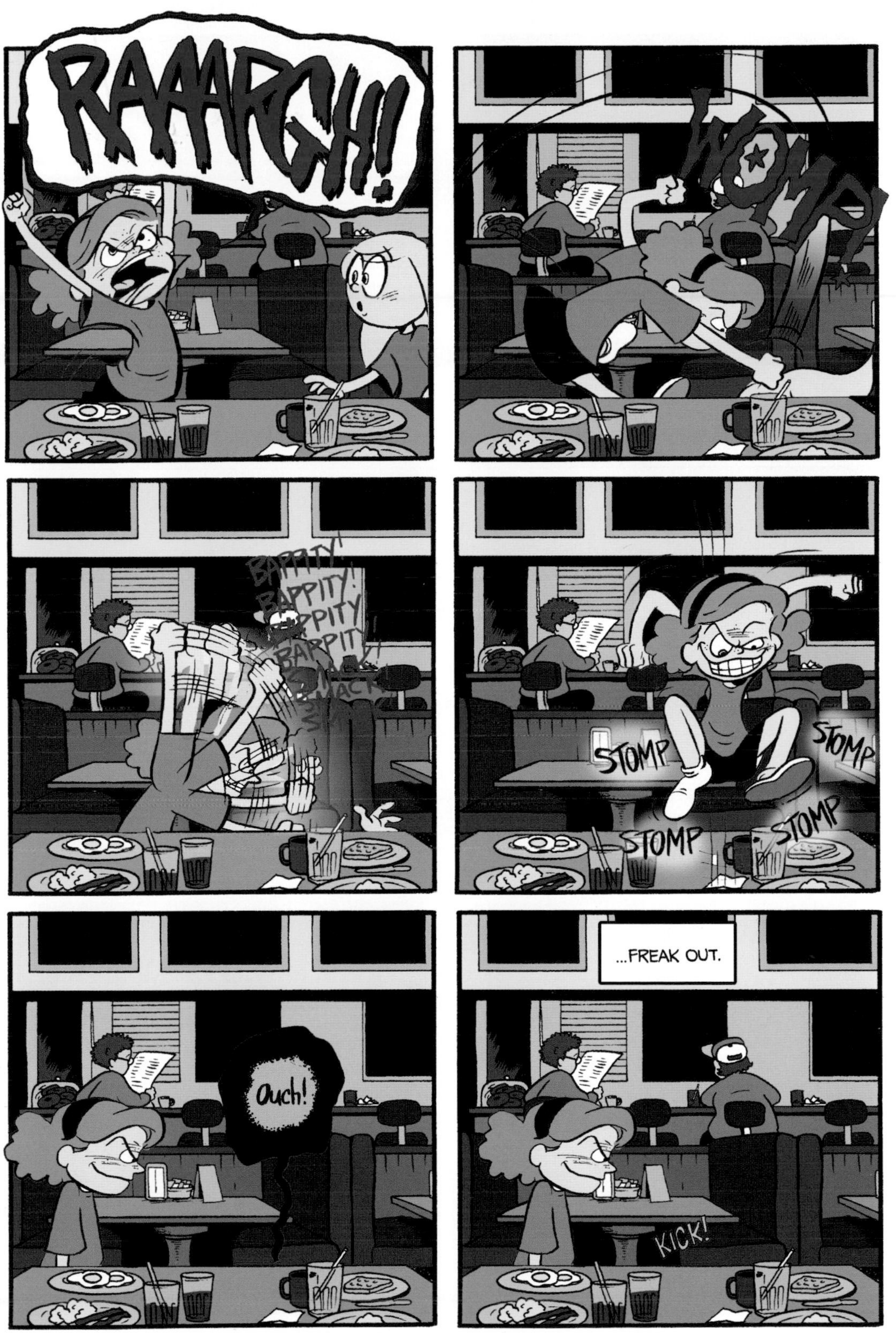
RAAARGH!!
WOMP
BAPPITY!
BAPPITY!
BAPPITY
BAPPITY
STOMP
STOMP!
STOMP
STOMP
Ouch!
...FREAK OUT.
KICK!

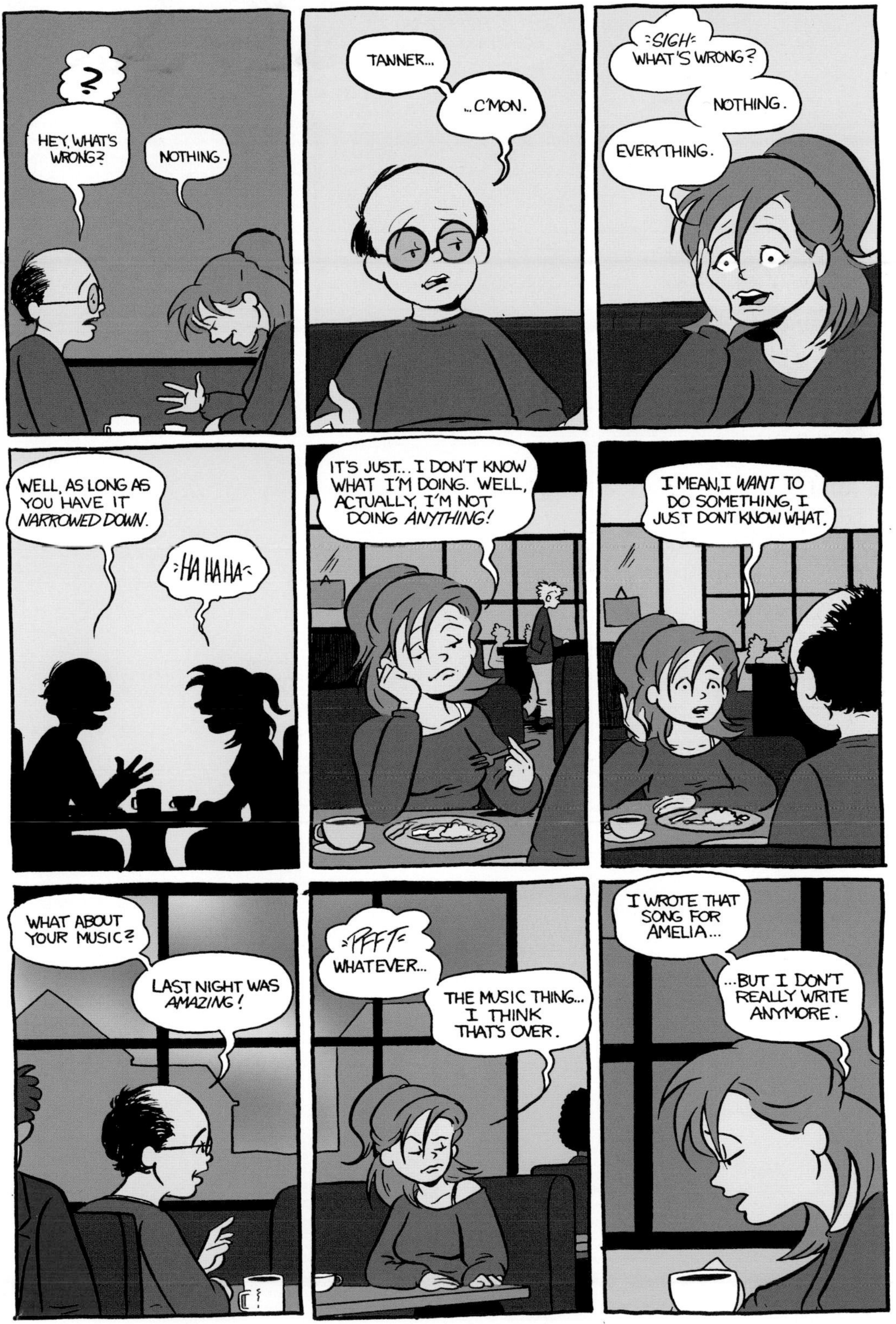
?
HEY, WHAT'S WRONG?
NOTHING.
TANNER...
...C'MON.
SIGH
WHAT'S WRONG?
NOTHING.
EVERYTHING.
WELL, AS LONG AS YOU HAVE IT NARROWED DOWN.
HA HA HA
IT'S JUST... I DON'T KNOW WHAT I'M DOING. WELL, ACTUALLY, I'M NOT DOING ANYTHING!
I MEAN, I WANT TO DO SOMETHING, I JUST DON'T KNOW WHAT.
WHAT ABOUT YOUR MUSIC?
LAST NIGHT WAS AMAZING!
PFFT
WHATEVER...
THE MUSIC THING... I THINK THAT'S OVER.
I WROTE THAT SONG FOR AMELIA...
...BUT I DON'T REALLY WRITE ANYMORE.

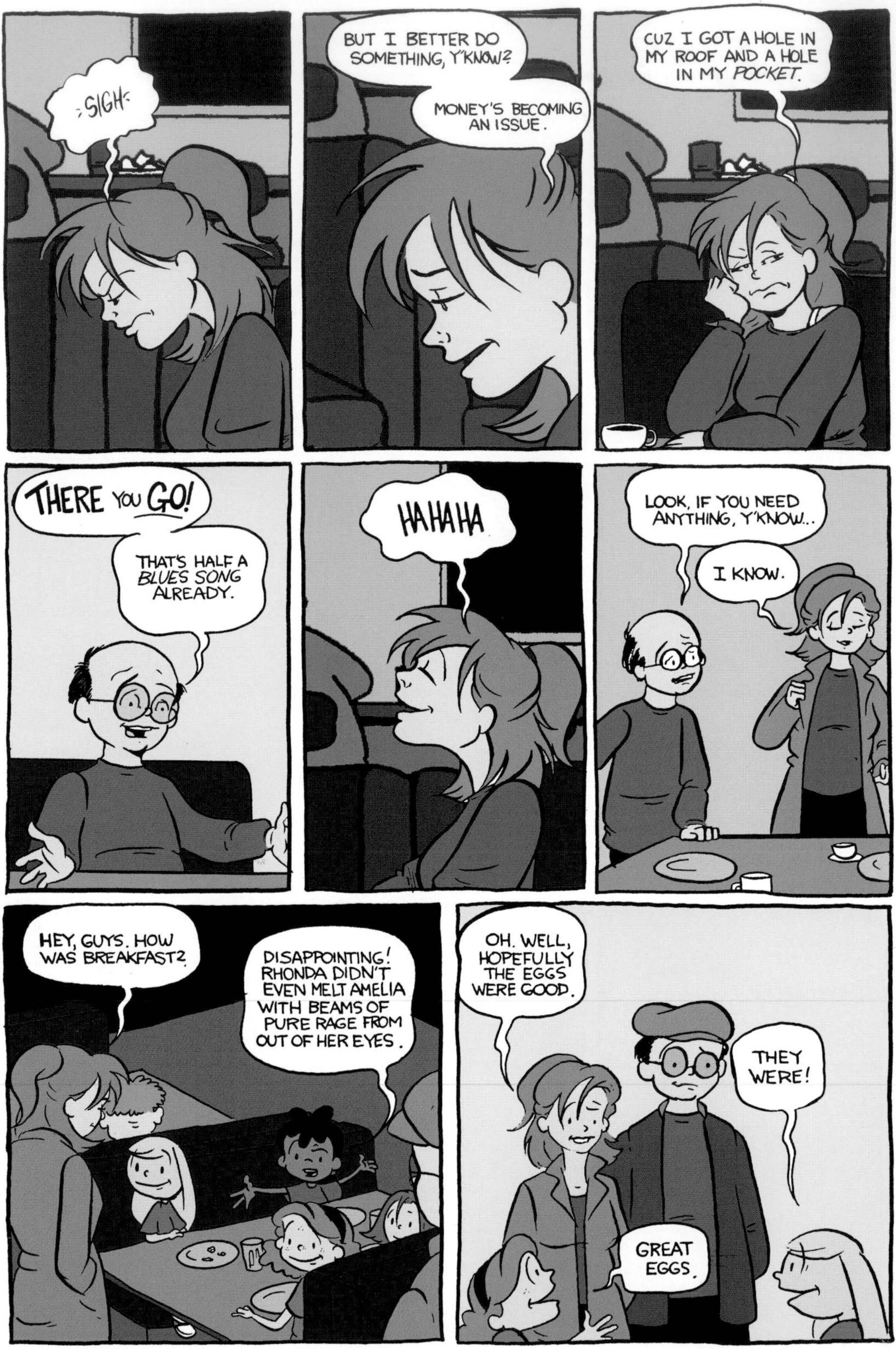
SIGH
BUT I BETTER DO SOMETHING, Y'KNOW?
MONEY'S BECOMING AN ISSUE.
CUZ I GOT A HOLE IN MY ROOF AND A HOLE IN MY POCKET.
THERE YOU GO!
THAT'S HALF A BLUES SONG ALREADY.
HAHAHA
LOOK, IF YOU NEED ANYTHING, Y'KNOW...
I KNOW.
HEY, GUYS. HOW WAS BREAKFAST?
DISAPPOINTING! RHONDA DIDN'T EVEN MELT AMELIA WITH BEAMS OF PURE RAGE FROM OUT OF HER EYES.
OH. WELL, HOPEFULLY THE EGGS WERE GOOD.
THEY WERE!
GREAT EGGS.

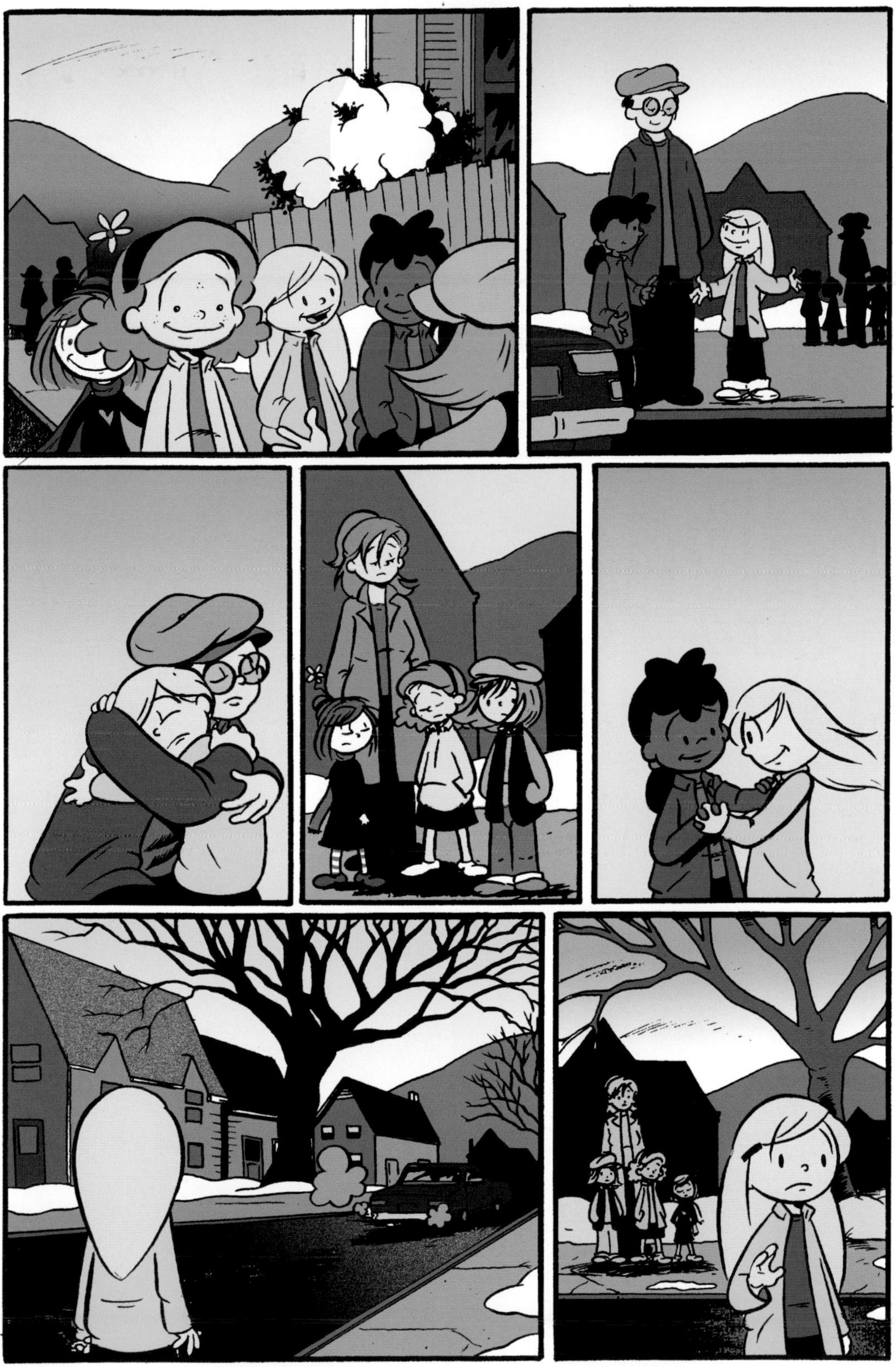

56

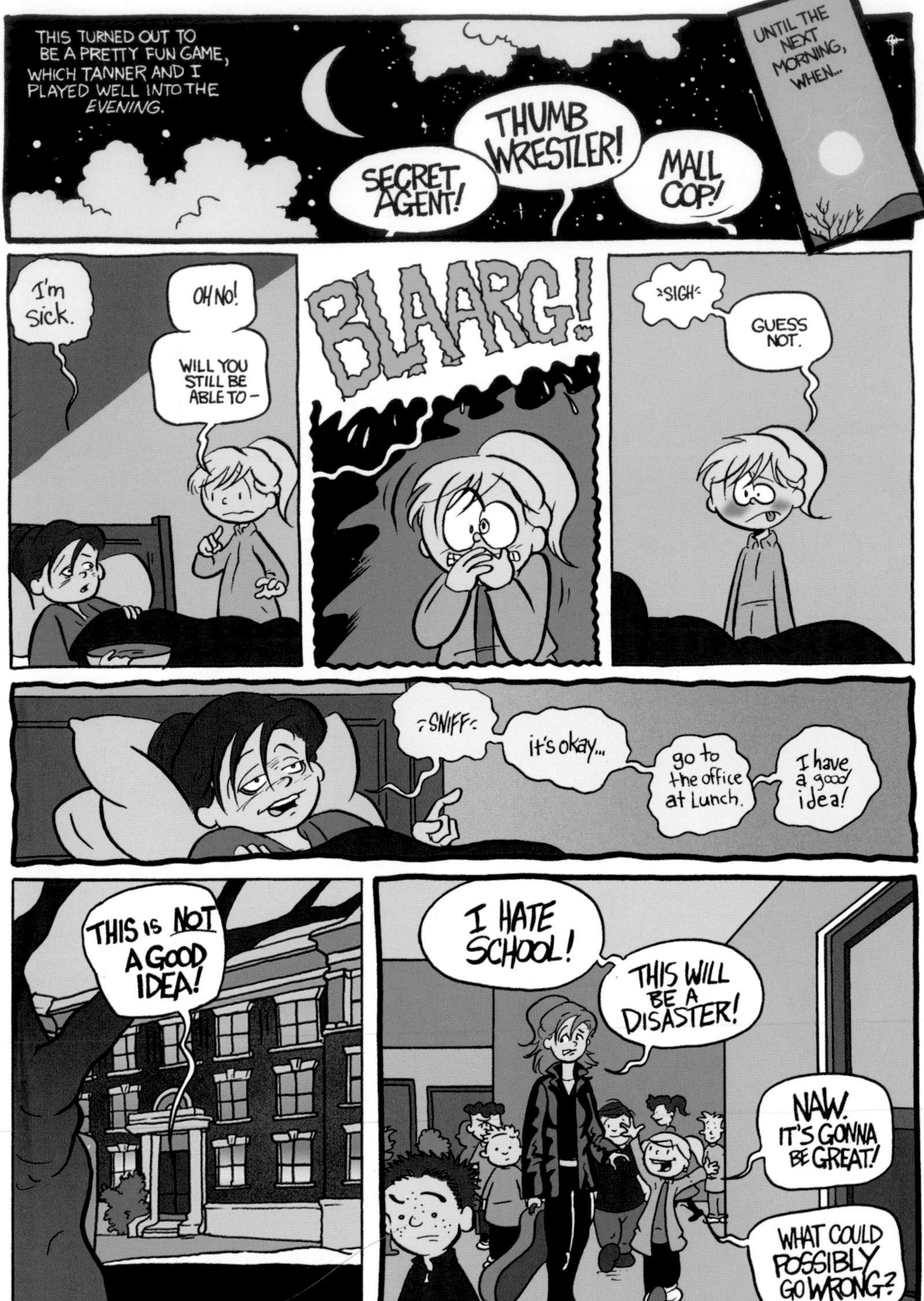

THIS TURNED OUT TO BE A PRETTY FUN GAME, WHICH TANNER AND I PLAYED WELL INTO THE EVENING.
SECRET AGENT!
THUMB WRESTLER!
MALL COP!
UNTIL THE NEXT MORNING, WHEN...
I'm sick.
OH NO!
WILL YOU STILL BE ABLE TO-
BLAARG!
SIGH
GUESS NOT.
SNIFF
it's okay...
go to the office at lunch.
I have a good idea!
THIS IS NOT A GOOD IDEA!
I HATE SCHOOL!
THIS WILL BE A DISASTER!
NAW. IT'S GONNA BE GREAT!
WHAT COULD POSSIBLY GO WRONG?

ACTUALLY, I COULD THINK OF LIKE *FORTY-SIX* THINGS THAT COULD GO WRONG, AND, LIKE, SEVEN THAT WOULD END WITH US AS THE TOP STORY ON FOX NEWS. ANYWAY, THE DAY WAS SUPER BORING! TANNER WENT LAST, BEHIND A DENTIST, A POLICE MAN, AND TWO WEBMASTERS. BUT THEN, *FINALLY*...

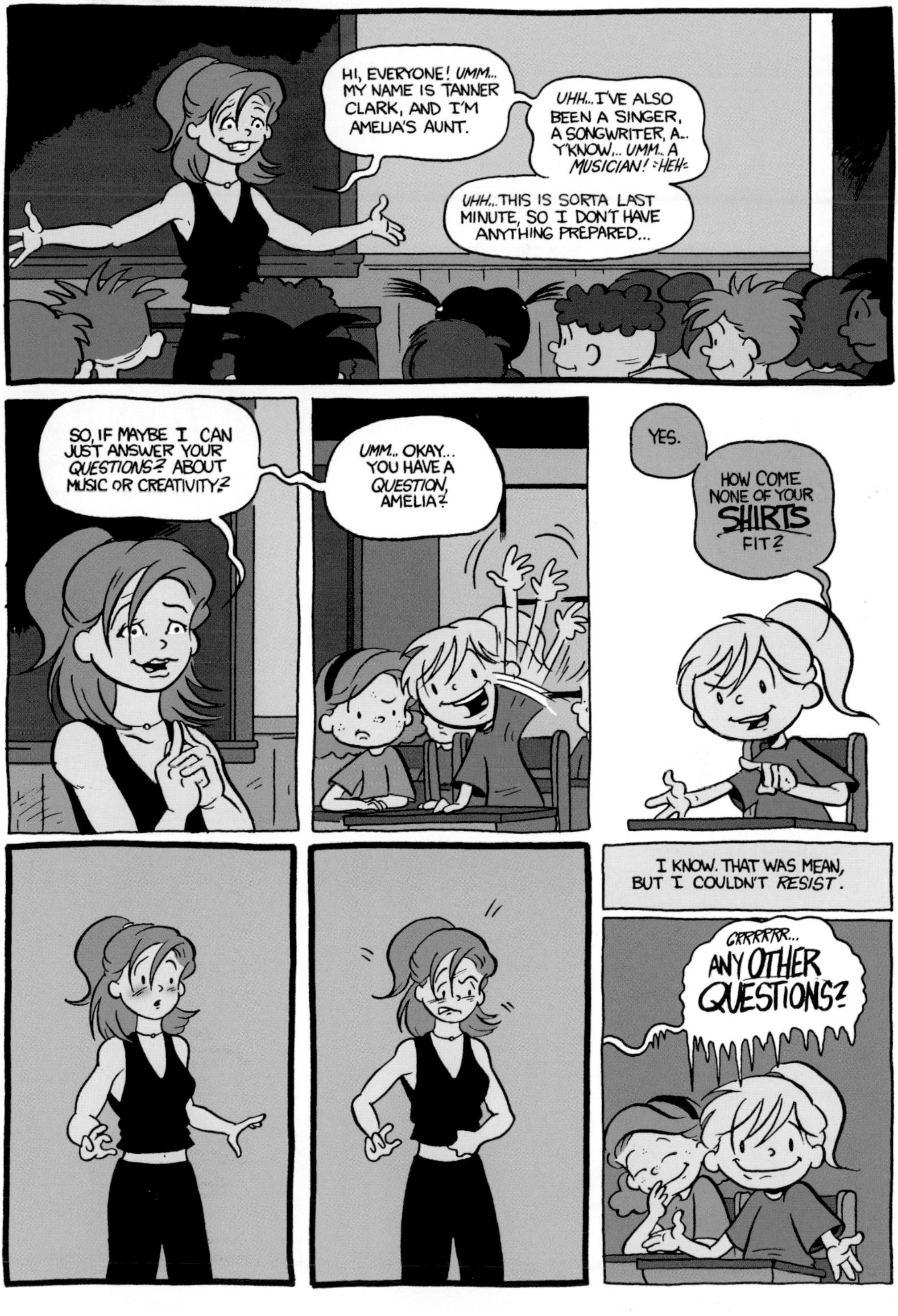
HI, EVERYONE! UMM... MY NAME IS TANNER CLARK, AND I'M AMELIA'S AUNT.
UHH... I'VE ALSO BEEN A SINGER, A SONGWRITER, A... Y'KNOW... UMM... A MUSICIAN! =HEH=
UHH... THIS IS SORTA LAST MINUTE, SO I DON'T HAVE ANYTHING PREPARED...
SO, IF MAYBE I CAN JUST ANSWER YOUR QUESTIONS? ABOUT MUSIC OR CREATIVITY?
UMM... OKAY... YOU HAVE A QUESTION, AMELIA?
YES.
HOW COME NONE OF YOUR SHIRTS FIT?
I KNOW. THAT WAS MEAN, BUT I COULDN'T RESIST.
GRRRRRR...
ANY OTHER QUESTIONS?

AND FOR A SECOND THINGS LOOKED *BAD*, BUT TANNER PULLED IT TOGETHER, AND SUDDENLY... *POW!*

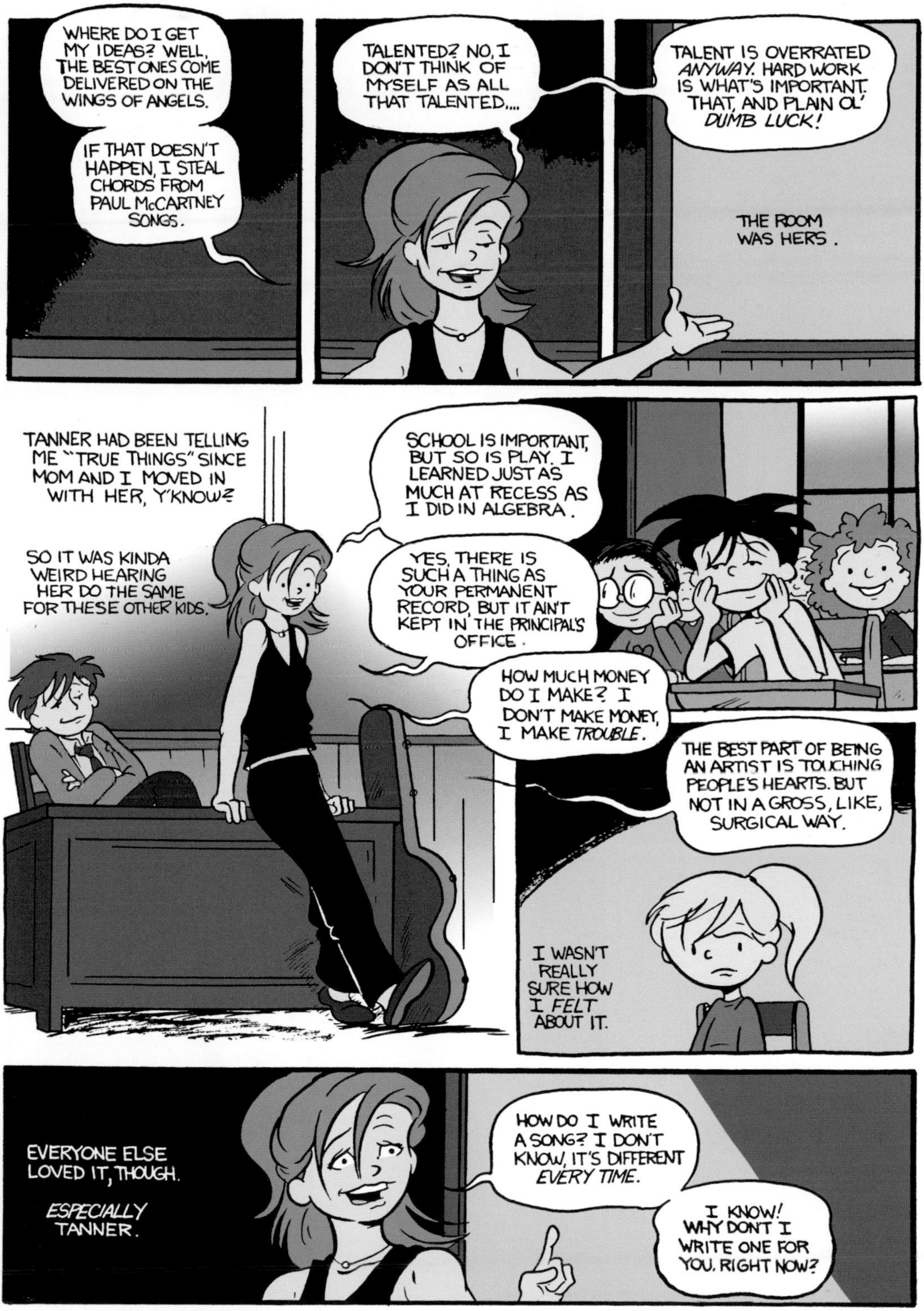
WHERE DO I GET MY IDEAS? WELL, THE BEST ONES COME DELIVERED ON THE WINGS OF ANGELS.
IF THAT DOESN'T HAPPEN, I STEAL CHORDS FROM PAUL McCARTNEY SONGS.
TALENTED? NO, I DON'T THINK OF MYSELF AS ALL THAT TALENTED....
TALENT IS OVERRATED *ANYWAY*. HARD WORK IS WHAT'S IMPORTANT. THAT, AND PLAIN OL' *DUMB LUCK!*
THE ROOM WAS HERS.
TANNER HAD BEEN TELLING ME "TRUE THINGS" SINCE MOM AND I MOVED IN WITH HER, Y'KNOW?
SO IT WAS KINDA WEIRD HEARING HER DO THE SAME FOR THESE OTHER KIDS.
SCHOOL IS IMPORTANT, BUT SO IS PLAY. I LEARNED JUST AS MUCH AT RECESS AS I DID IN ALGEBRA.
YES, THERE IS SUCH A THING AS YOUR PERMANENT RECORD, BUT IT AIN'T KEPT IN THE PRINCIPAL'S OFFICE.
HOW MUCH MONEY DO I MAKE? I DON'T MAKE MONEY, I MAKE *TROUBLE*.
THE BEST PART OF BEING AN ARTIST IS TOUCHING PEOPLE'S HEARTS. BUT NOT IN A GROSS, LIKE, SURGICAL WAY.
I WASN'T REALLY SURE HOW I *FELT* ABOUT IT.
EVERYONE ELSE LOVED IT, THOUGH.
ESPECIALLY TANNER.
HOW DO I WRITE A SONG? I DON'T KNOW, IT'S DIFFERENT *EVERY TIME*.
I KNOW! WHY DON'T I WRITE ONE FOR YOU, RIGHT NOW?

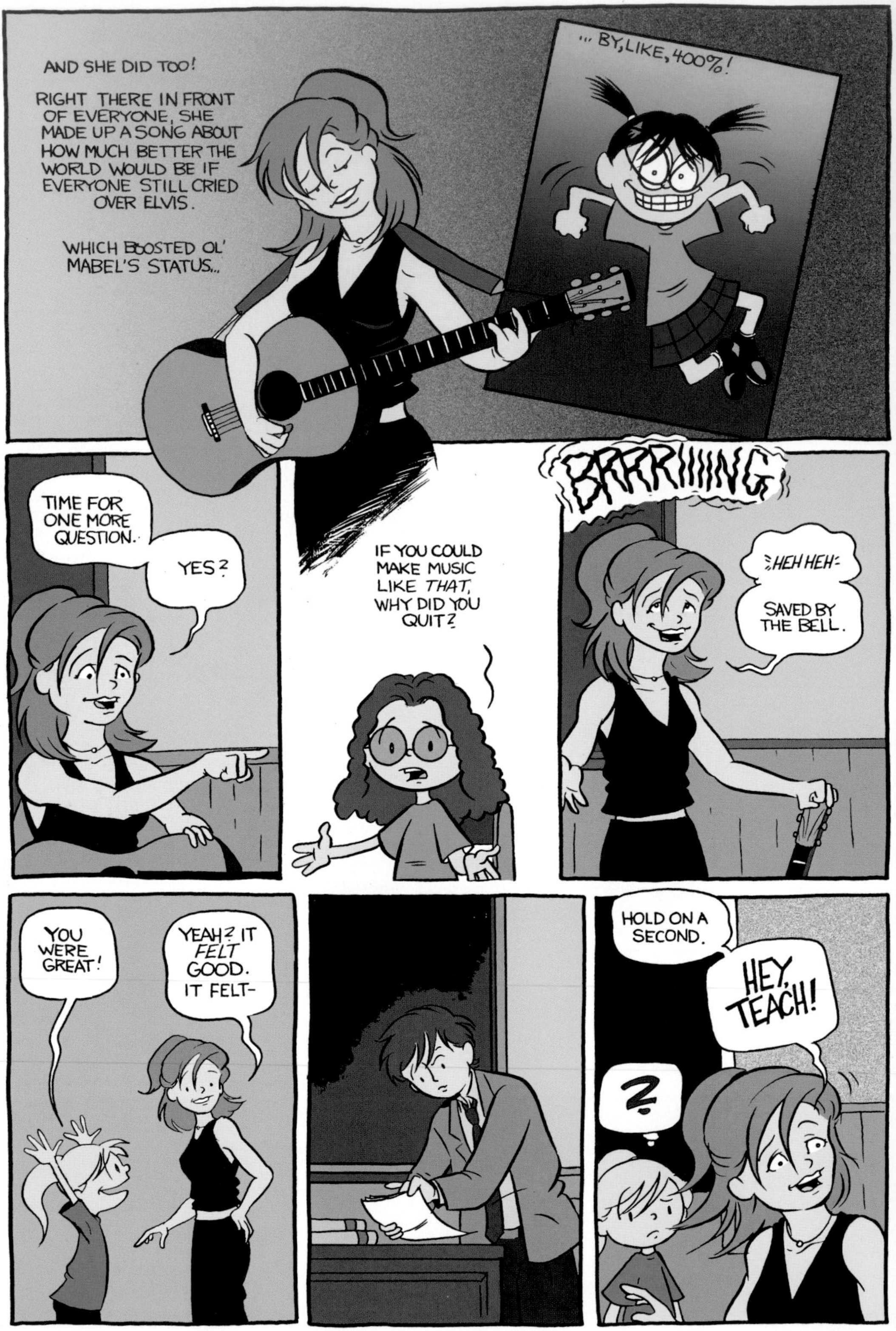
AND SHE DID TOO!
RIGHT THERE IN FRONT OF EVERYONE, SHE MADE UP A SONG ABOUT HOW MUCH BETTER THE WORLD WOULD BE IF EVERYONE STILL CRIED OVER ELVIS.
WHICH BOOSTED OL' MABEL'S STATUS...
... BY, LIKE, 400%!
TIME FOR ONE MORE QUESTION.
YES?
IF YOU COULD MAKE MUSIC LIKE *THAT*, WHY DID YOU QUIT?
BRRRIIIING
HEH HEH
SAVED BY THE BELL.
YOU WERE GREAT!
YEAH? IT *FELT* GOOD. IT FELT-
HOLD ON A SECOND.
HEY, TEACH!
?

63

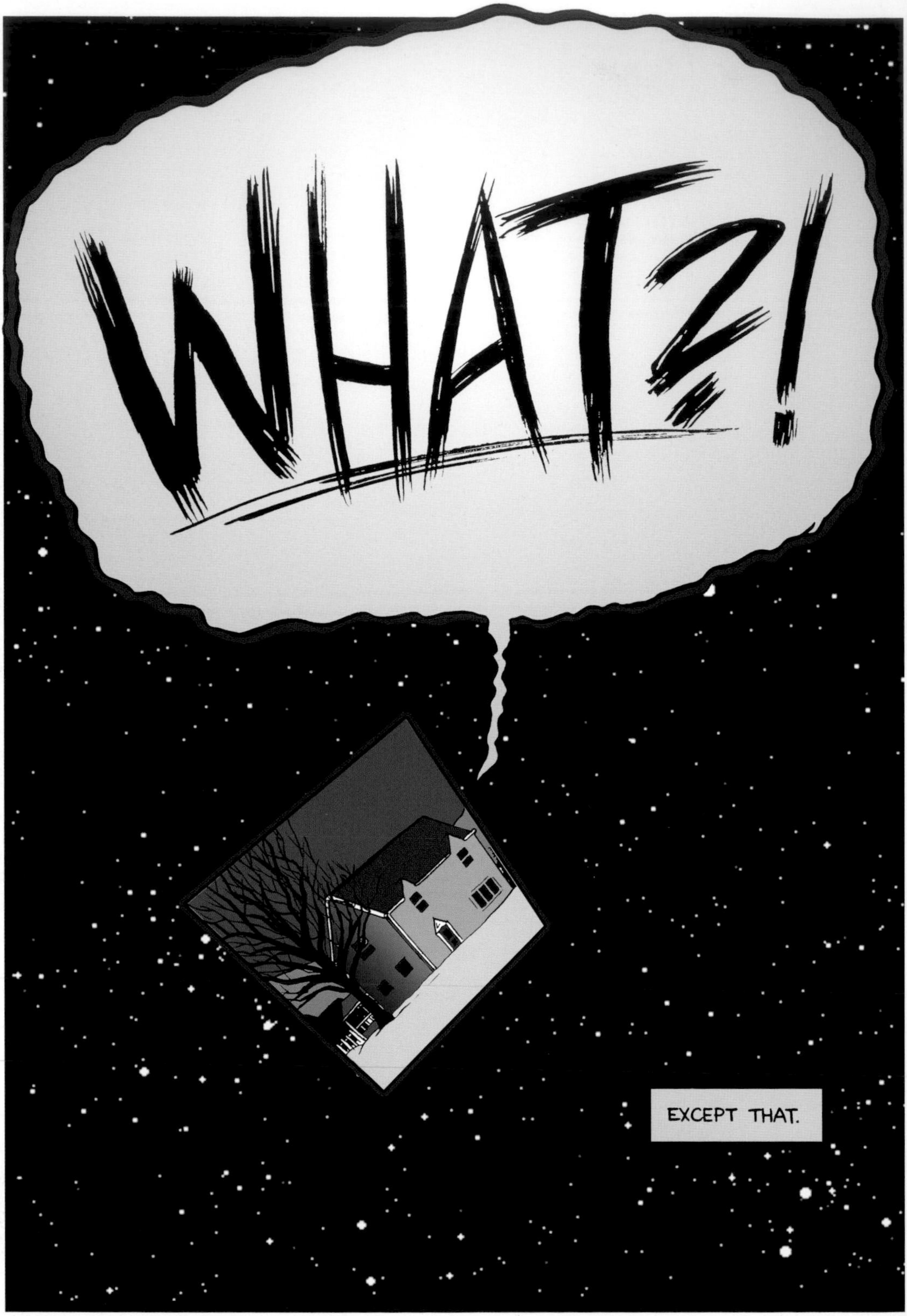
WHAT?!
EXCEPT THAT.

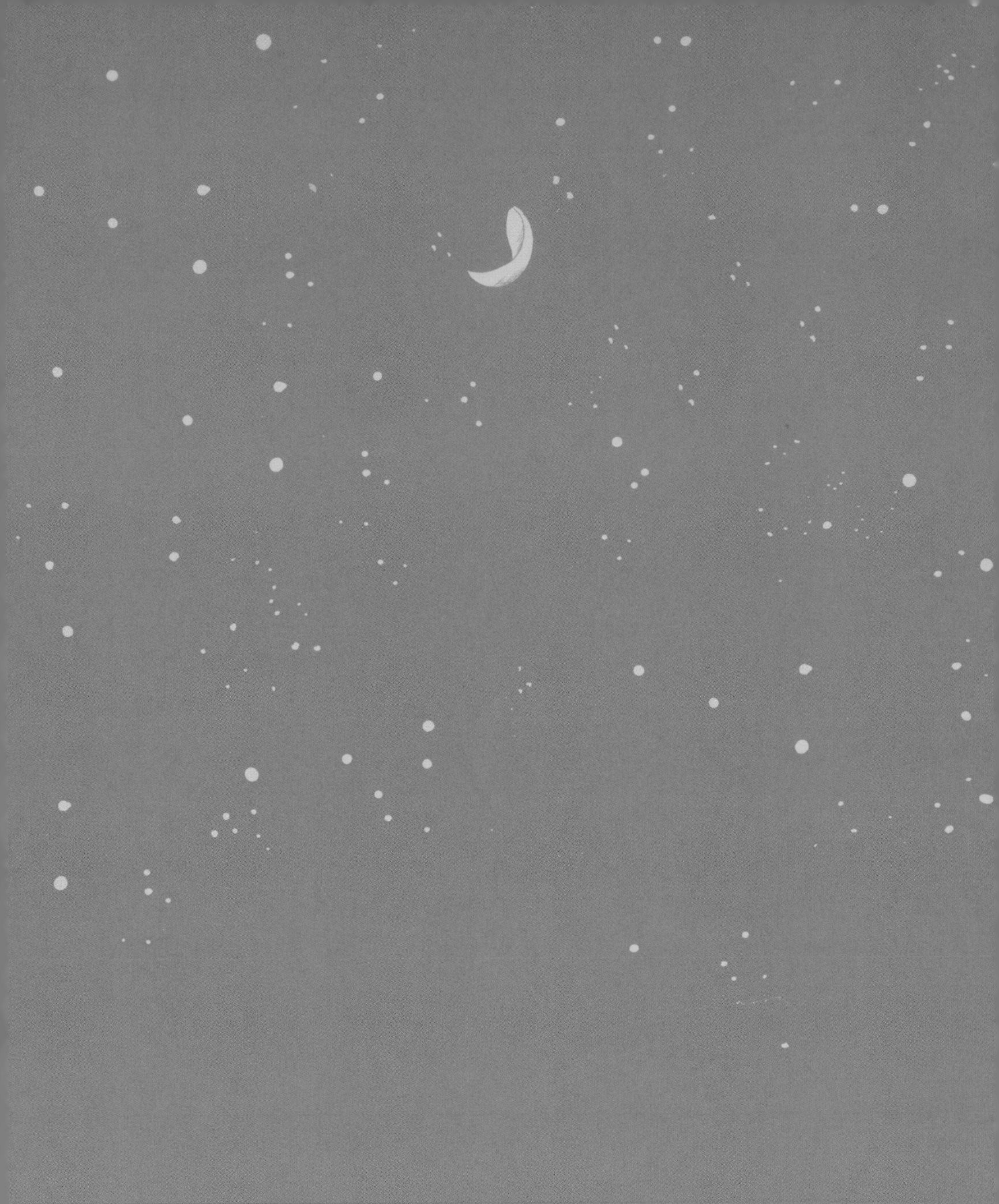

"I think the reason people have kids is so they can pass their own brand of crazy on to a new generation."

-Tanner Clark

in an Interview with Chet McCoy of *Good Morning St. Louis*

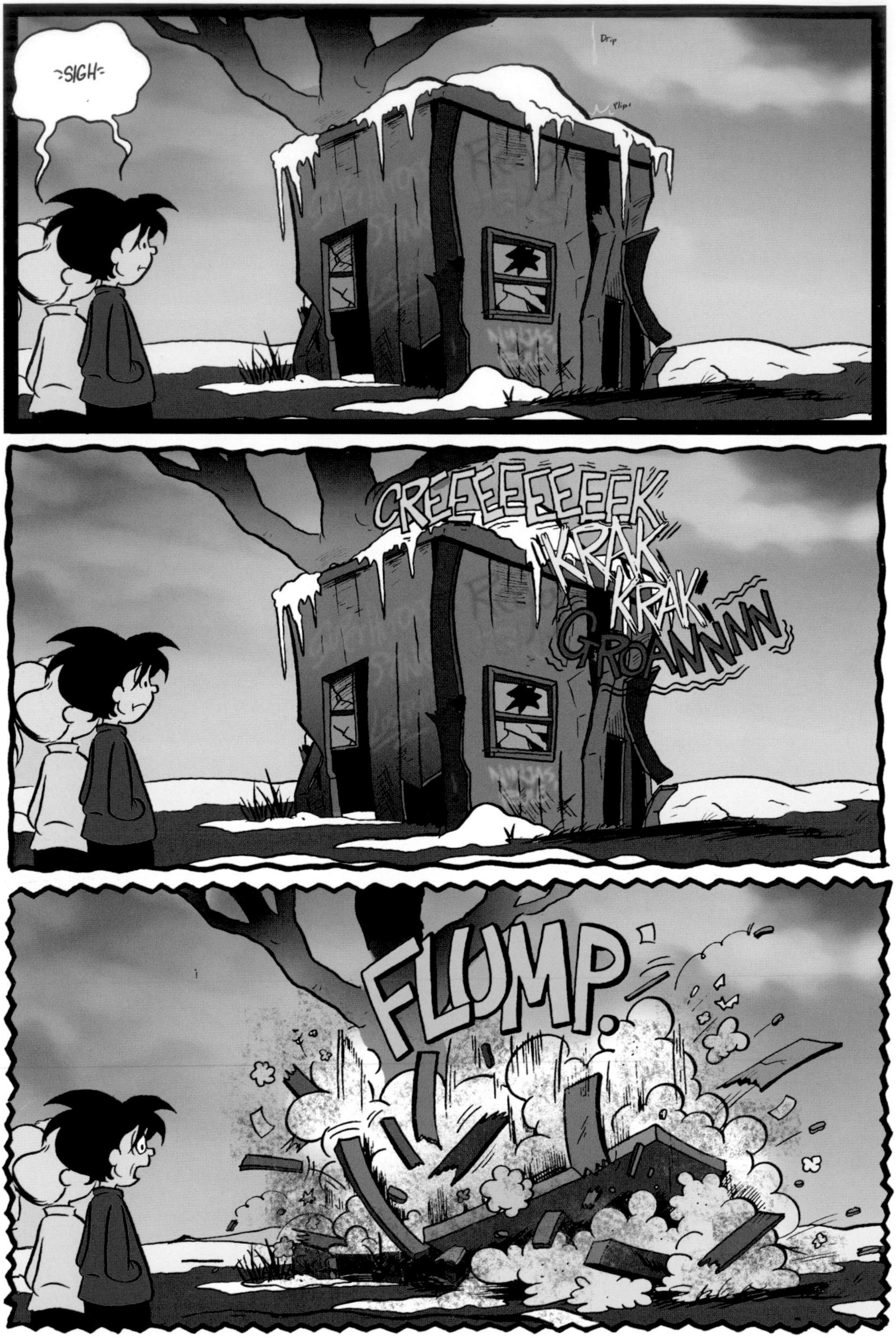
SIGH
Drip
Plip
CREEEEEEEEK
KRAK
KRAK
GROANNNNN
FLUMP.

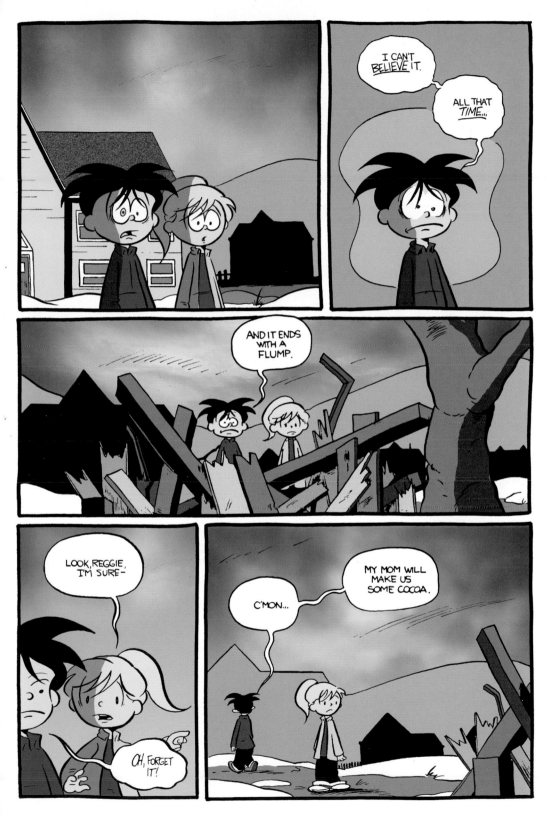

82

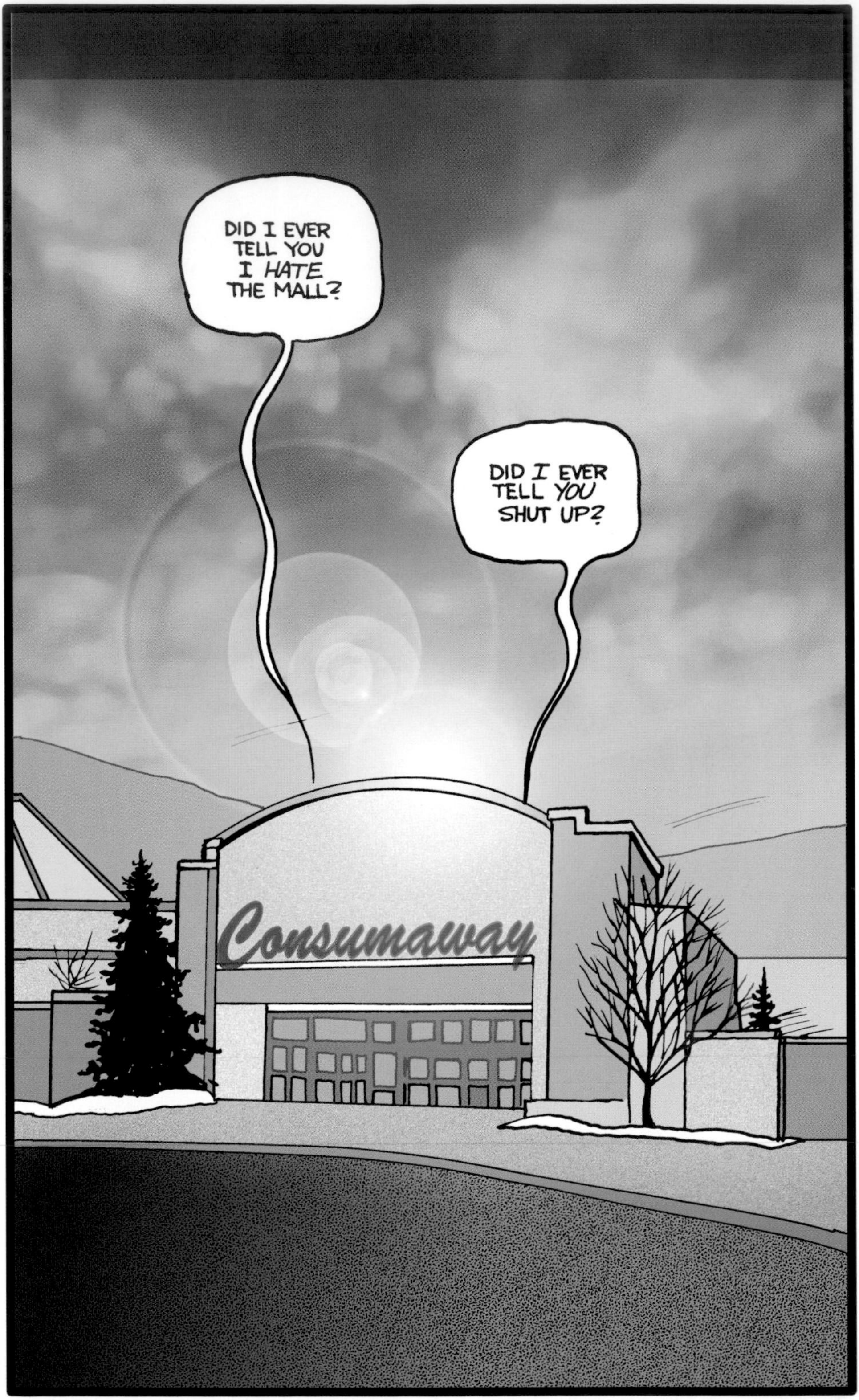
DID I EVER TELL YOU I HATE THE MALL?
DID I EVER TELL YOU SHUT UP?
Consumaway

88

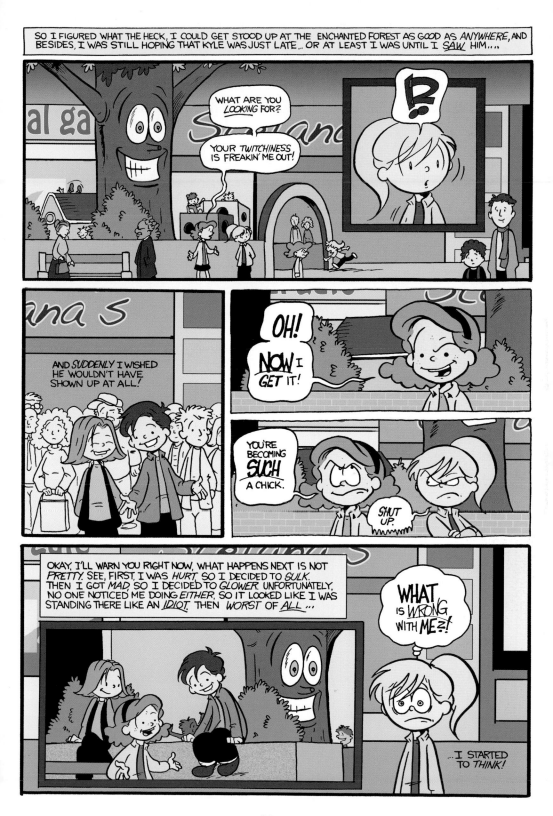

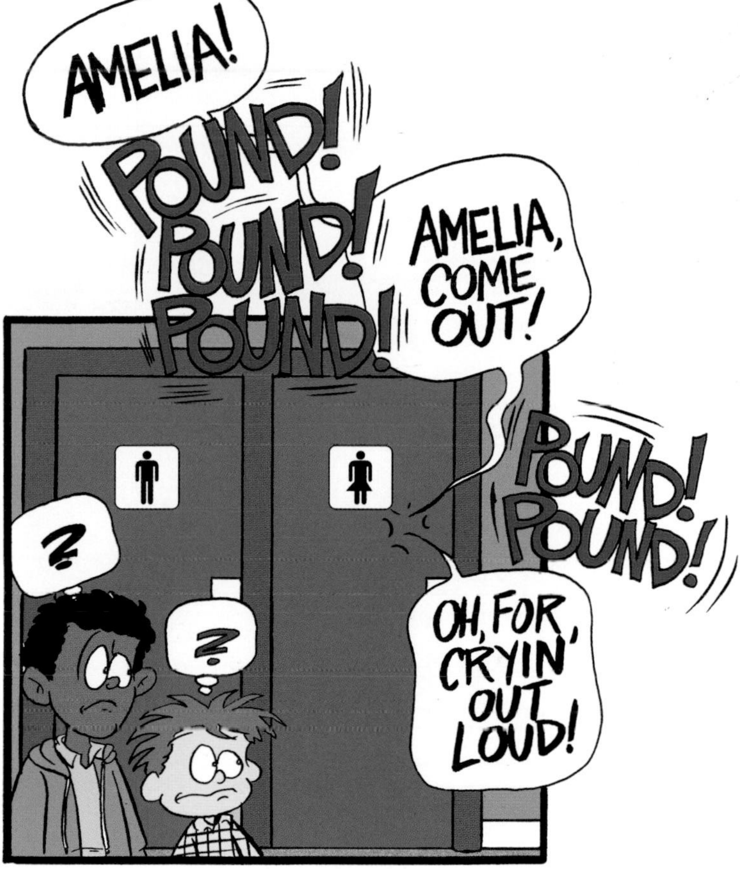
AMELIA!
POUND! POUND! POUND!
AMELIA, COME OUT!
POUND! POUND!
?
?
OH, FOR, CRYIN' OUT LOUD!

94

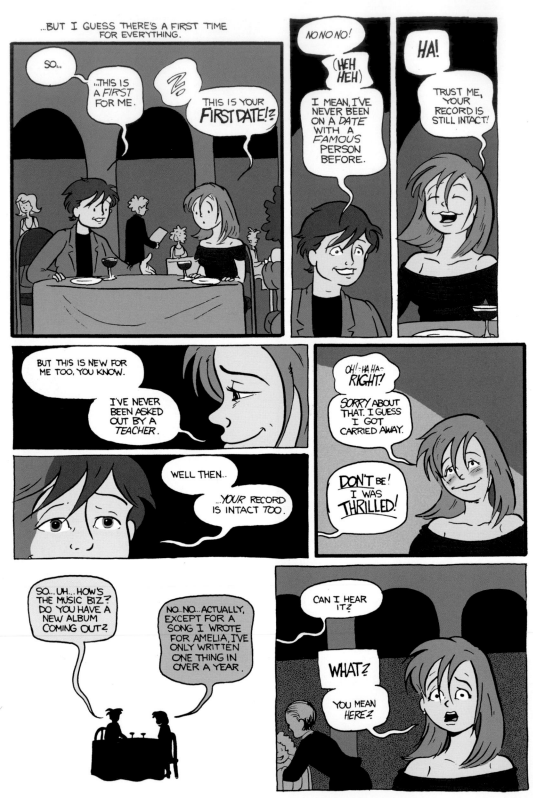

97

99

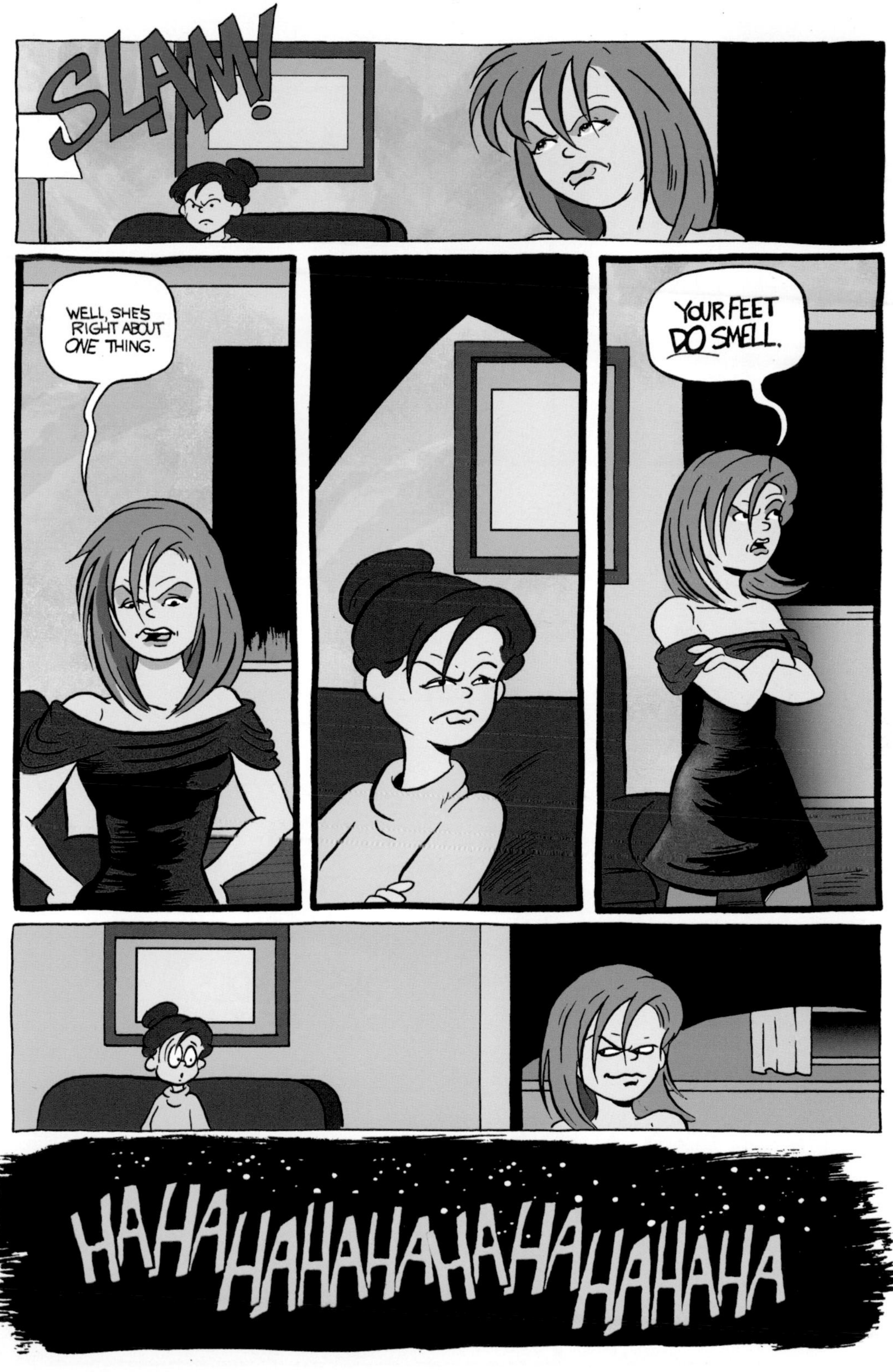
SLAM!
WELL, SHE'S RIGHT ABOUT ONE THING.
YOUR FEET DO SMELL.
HAHAHAHAHAHAHAHAHAHAHAHAHAHAHA

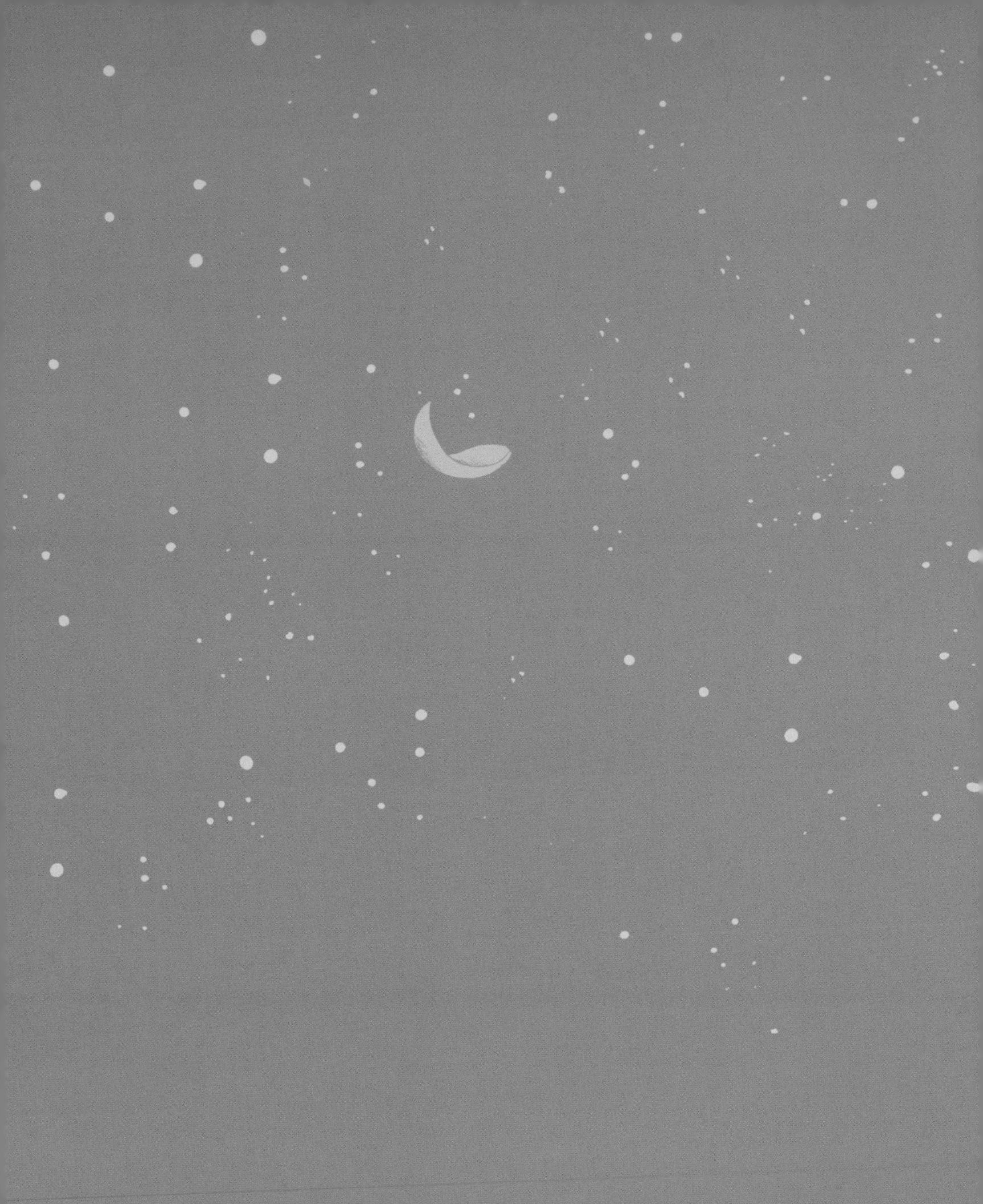

"Art is like a beautiful dream, and the rest of the world is the alarm clock."

-Tanner Clark

from the liner notes of *Broken Record*

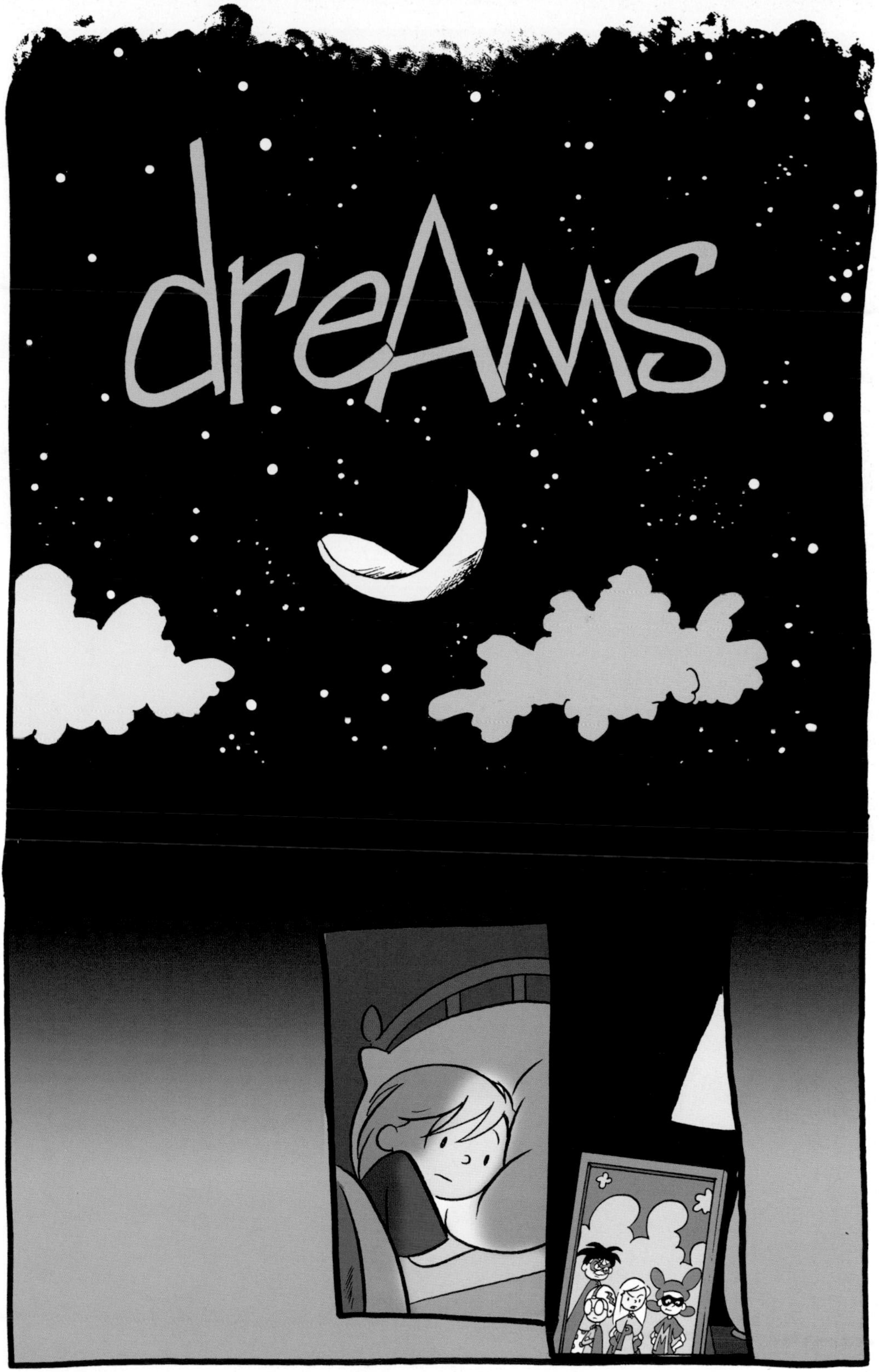
dreAms

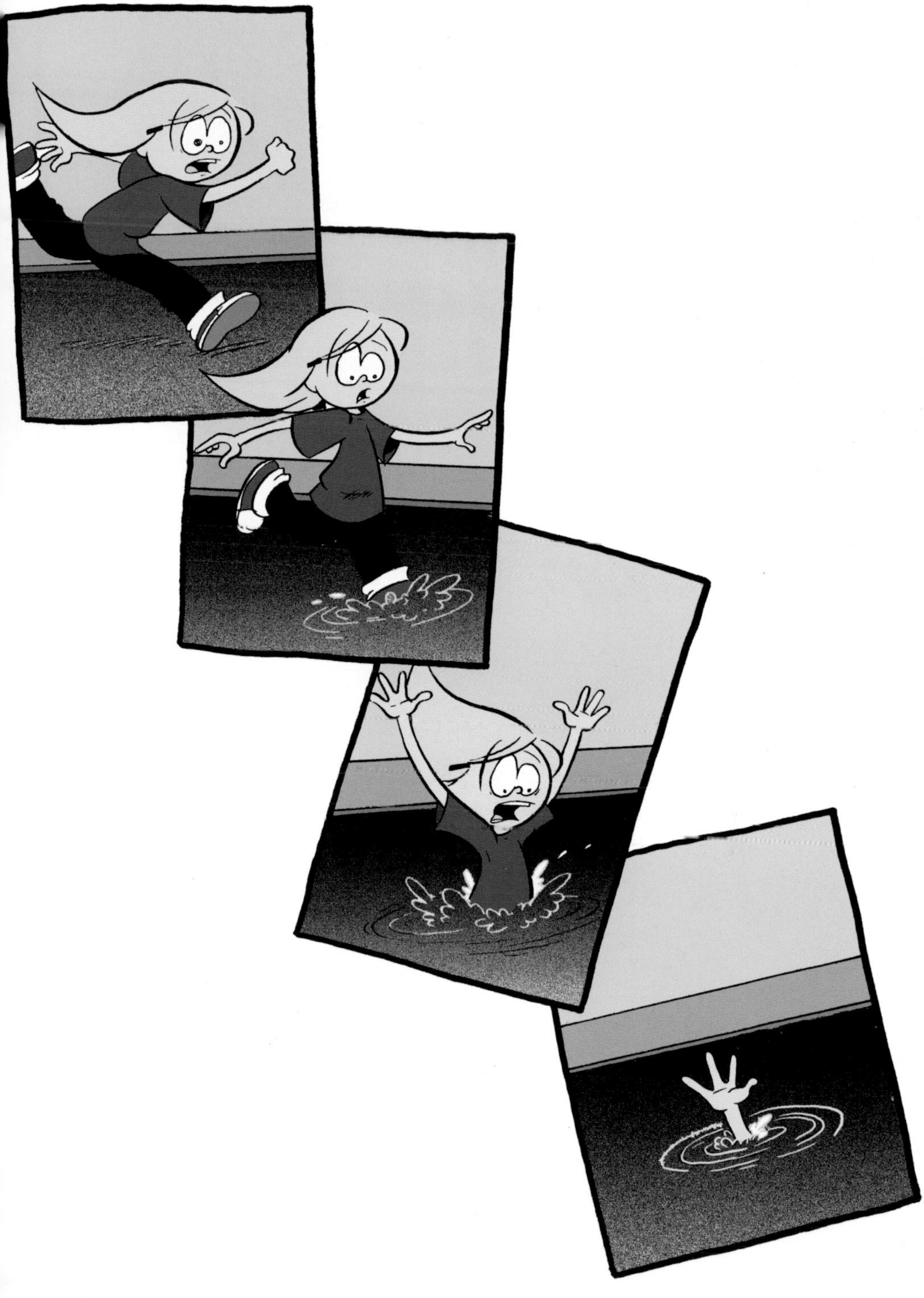

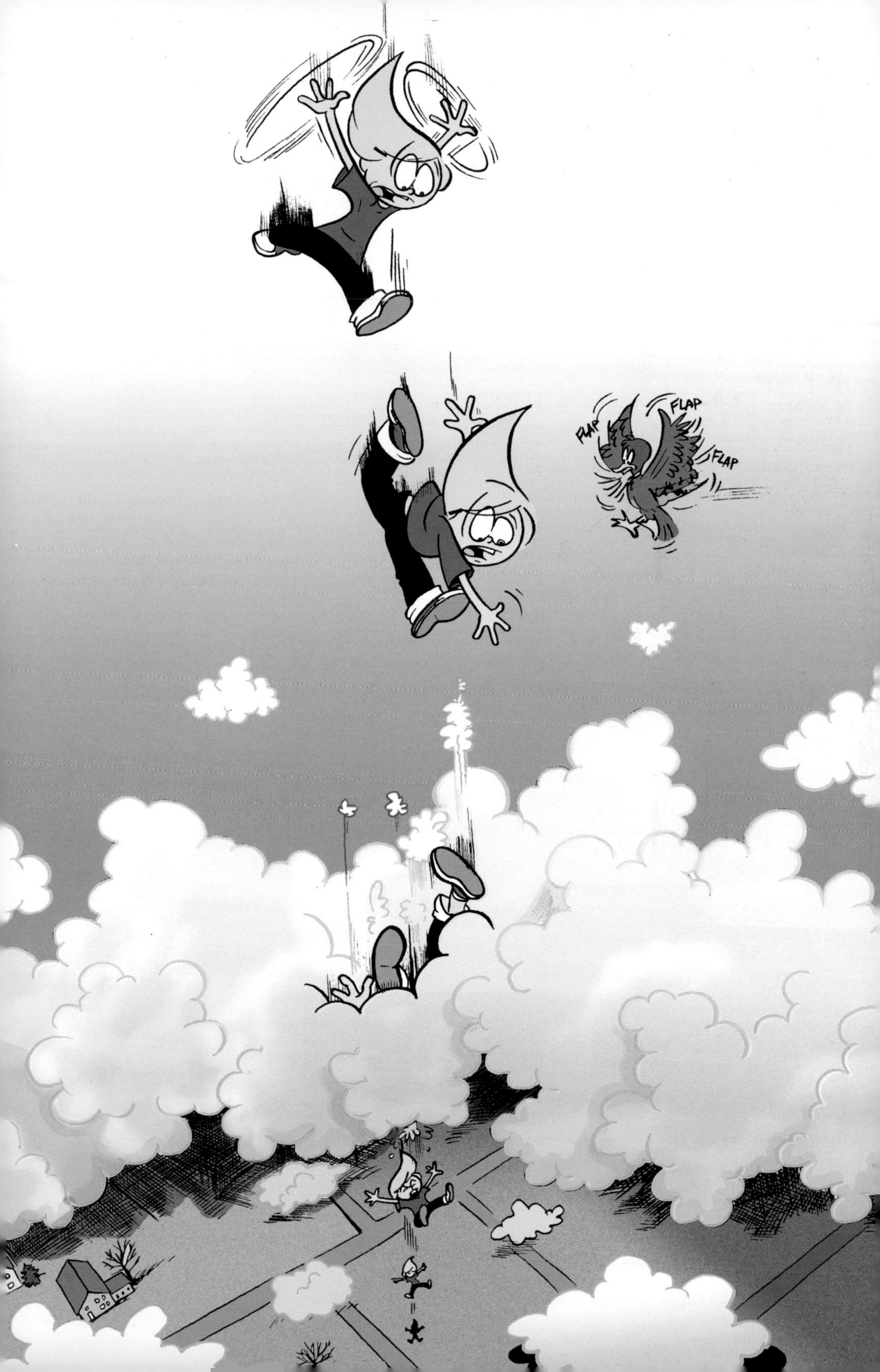
FLAP
FLAP
FLAP

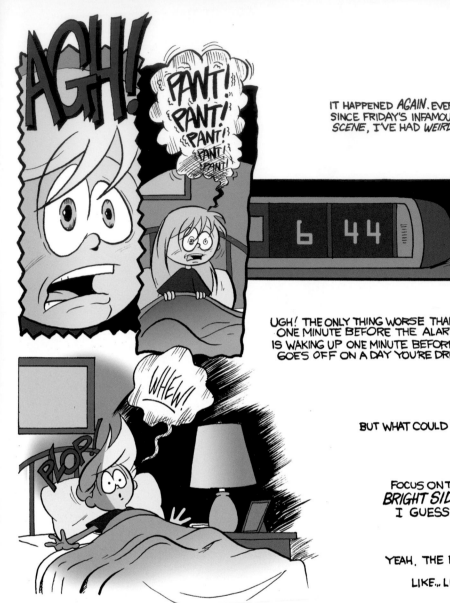

IT HAPPENED *AGAIN*. EVERY NIGHT SINCE FRIDAY'S INFAMOUS *MALL SCENE*, I'VE HAD *WEIRD DREAMS*.

UGH! THE ONLY THING WORSE THAN WAKING UP ONE MINUTE BEFORE THE ALARM GOES OFF IS WAKING UP ONE MINUTE BEFORE THE ALARM GOES OFF ON A DAY YOU'RE DREADING, ANYWAY.

BUT WHAT COULD I DO?

FOCUS ON THE *BRIGHT SIDE*, I GUESS.

YEAH. THE BRIGHT SIDE.

LIKE... LIKE...

HMM...

OH!

HERE'S SOMETHING...

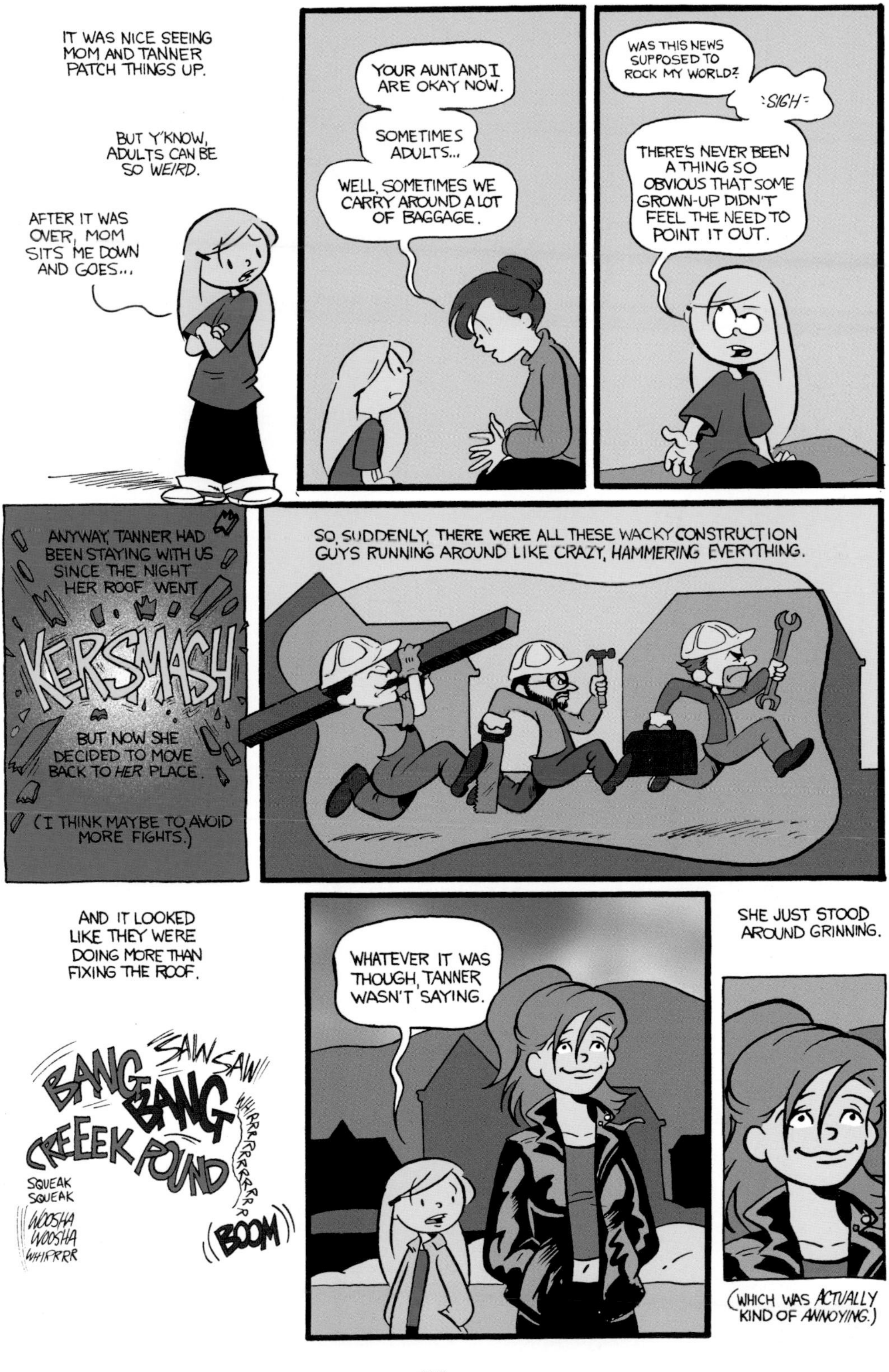
IT WAS NICE SEEING MOM AND TANNER PATCH THINGS UP.
BUT Y'KNOW, ADULTS CAN BE SO WEIRD.
AFTER IT WAS OVER, MOM SITS ME DOWN AND GOES...
YOUR AUNT AND I ARE OKAY NOW.
SOMETIMES ADULTS...
WELL, SOMETIMES WE CARRY AROUND A LOT OF BAGGAGE.
WAS THIS NEWS SUPPOSED TO ROCK MY WORLD?
SIGH
THERE'S NEVER BEEN A THING SO OBVIOUS THAT SOME GROWN-UP DIDN'T FEEL THE NEED TO POINT IT OUT.
ANYWAY, TANNER HAD BEEN STAYING WITH US SINCE THE NIGHT HER ROOF WENT
KERSMASH
BUT NOW SHE DECIDED TO MOVE BACK TO HER PLACE.
(I THINK MAYBE TO AVOID MORE FIGHTS.)
SO, SUDDENLY, THERE WERE ALL THESE WACKY CONSTRUCTION GUYS RUNNING AROUND LIKE CRAZY, HAMMERING EVERYTHING.
AND IT LOOKED LIKE THEY WERE DOING MORE THAN FIXING THE ROOF.
SAW SAW
BANG
BANG
CREEEK POUND
SQUEAK SQUEAK
WOOSHA WOOSHA
WHIRRRR
WHIRRRRRRRRRRR
BOOM
WHATEVER IT WAS THOUGH, TANNER WASN'T SAYING.
SHE JUST STOOD AROUND GRINNING.
(WHICH WAS ACTUALLY KIND OF ANNOYING.)

NOW, I GUESS THERE WERE **TWO** REASONS FOR TANNER TO BE GRINNING LIKE AN IDIOT.

ONE: WHATEVER WAS GOING ON INSIDE HER HOUSE,

CONSTRUCTION WISE,

AND...

TWO: MR. HENDERSON.

MR. *PETER* HENDERSON AS IT TURNS OUT.

("*PETE-O*," ACCORDING TO THE FREEWHEELIN' MS. CLARK!)

DON'T GET ME WRONG. I *LIKE* MR. HENDERSON A *LOT.*

HE'S A GOOD TEACHER.

TONS BETTER THAN THE *OTHER* JERKS I'VE HAD.

AS A MATTER OF FACT, *SOME* GIRLS IN MY CLASS EVEN HAD A *CRUSH* ON HIM.

-SIIIIIIGH-

NO, *NOT* ME.

I HAVE *ENOUGH* PROBLEMS, THANKS.

AND ANYWAY, THESE DAYS HE WAS 'HOGGIN' UP ALL OF TANNER'S TIME! IT WASN'T LIKE THEY WENT ON LOTS OF *DIFFERENT* DATES...

IT WAS LIKE THEY WENT ON ONE DATE THAT NEVER ENDED.

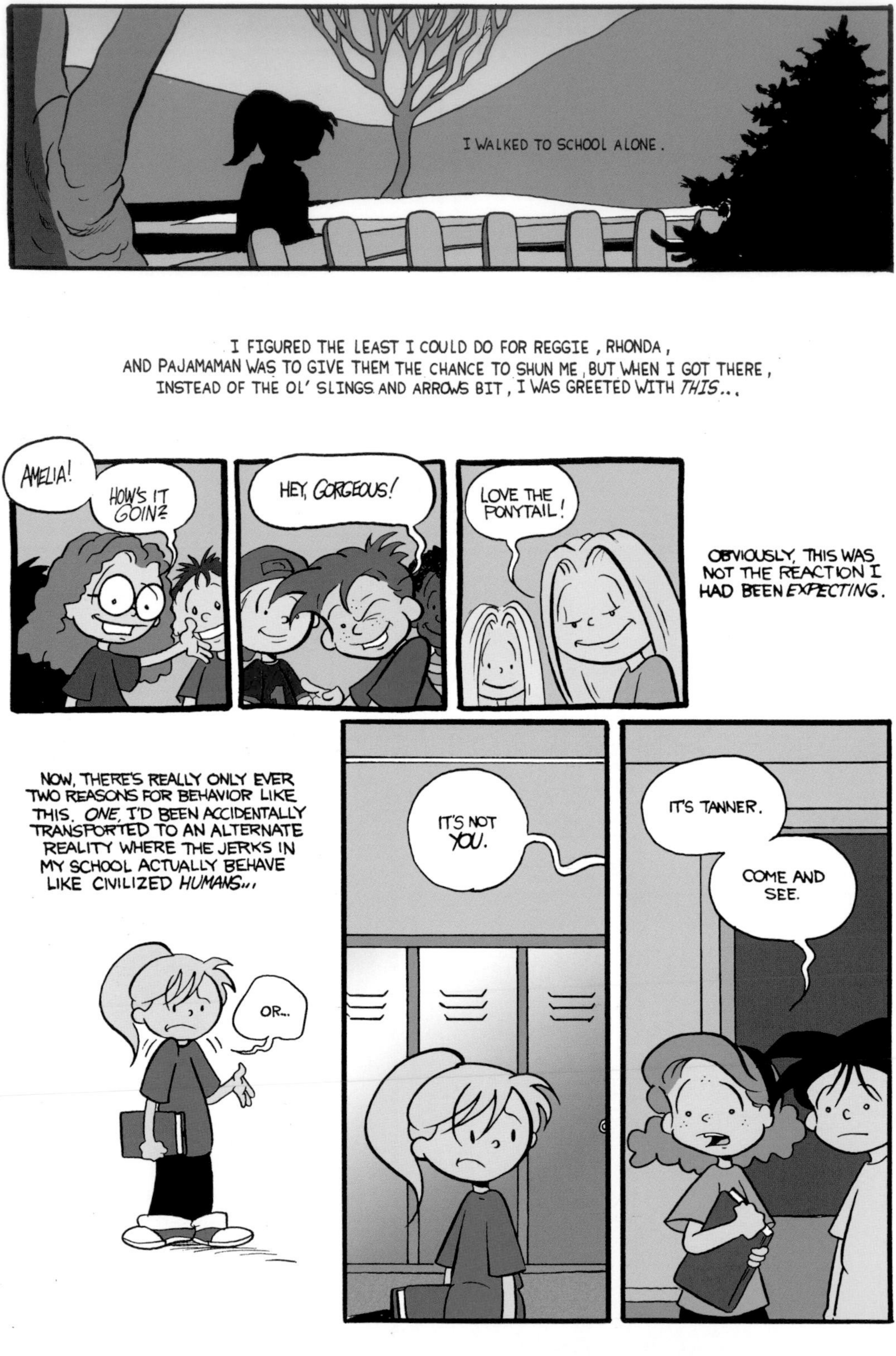
I WALKED TO SCHOOL ALONE.
I FIGURED THE LEAST I COULD DO FOR REGGIE, RHONDA, AND PAJAMAMAN WAS TO GIVE THEM THE CHANCE TO SHUN ME, BUT WHEN I GOT THERE, INSTEAD OF THE OL' SLINGS AND ARROWS BIT, I WAS GREETED WITH THIS...
AMELIA!
HOW'S IT GOIN?
HEY, GORGEOUS!
LOVE THE PONYTAIL!
OBVIOUSLY, THIS WAS NOT THE REACTION I HAD BEEN EXPECTING.
NOW, THERE'S REALLY ONLY EVER TWO REASONS FOR BEHAVIOR LIKE THIS. ONE, I'D BEEN ACCIDENTALLY TRANSPORTED TO AN ALTERNATE REALITY WHERE THE JERKS IN MY SCHOOL ACTUALLY BEHAVE LIKE CIVILIZED HUMANS...
OR...
IT'S NOT YOU.
IT'S TANNER.
COME AND SEE.

THEY DRAGGED ME INTO THE COMPUTER LAB WHERE WE COULD LOG ONTO THE INTERNET. THIS IS NOT ALLOWED AT OUR SCHOOL, BY THE WAY, WHICH MEANS EVERYONE DOES IT AS OFTEN AS POSSIBLE. THE PASSWORD IS, I SWEAR, "TEACHER." LUCKILY, OUR SCHOOL WAS NOT IN ANY WAY RESPONSIBLE FOR HOMELAND SECURITY.

ANYWAY...

THERE IT WAS... TWEENIEZEENIE.COM HAD A WHOLE WRITE-UP ON MY BIRTHDAY PARTY. WELL, MORE LIKE TANNER'S PERFORMANCE AT MY PARTY. HANNIGAN HAD EVEN UPLOADED THE SONG SHE PLAYED, AND GET THIS...

IT HAD BEEN DOWNLOADED, LIKE, 50,000 TIMES.

RIGHT THEN I REALIZED TWO THINGS: ONE, TANNER WAS STILL KINDA FAMOUS, AND TWO, I WAS DEFINITELY NOT GONNA TELL HER THAT MY FRIEND'S WEBSITE WAS BOOTLEGGING HER MUSIC.

TANNER CLARK
Plays private party!

DOWNLOAD SONG!

HEY, GUYS! WHAT'S UP?

OH.

HI, JOAN.

AND BY "JOAN," I MEAN...

"TRAITOR!"

"BENEDICT ARNOLD!"

"JERK!"

DOIEEE!

MY FEELINGS FOR JOAN DRISCOLL HAD GROWN... "COMPLEX" SINCE FRIDAY. I MEAN, IT'S NOT THAT I CARED THAT SHE WAS WITH KYLE.

WHY WOULD I? I JUST THINK IT'S RUDE TO BE WITH SOMEONE WHEN THAT SOMEONE WAS SUPPOSE TO BE WITH ANOTHER SOMEONE, EVEN THOUGH THAT SOMEONE COULDN'T CARE LESS.

119

OKAY, SO THAT WAS *TWO* THINGS OFF THE OL' *GRAY MATTER*. *ONE*, JOAN WAS NOT INTO *KYLE!* (NOT THAT *I* CARE!)

AND *TWO*, THE SCHOOL WAS NOT AS INTERESTED IN MY *FOOT* AND/OR INTESTINAL ISSUES AS I *THOUGHT* THEY *WOULD* BE!

PLUS...

...ON TOP OF THOSE NICE SURPRISES, IN ENGLISH CLASS, WE GOT A NEW ASSIGNMENT... *JOURNAL WRITING*.

HOW COOL IS *THAT*!

SELF-OBSESSED WHINING AS A WAY TO BOOST A GRADE POINT AVERAGE? *SIGN* ME *UP!*

JOURNAL WRITING CAN BE A *GREAT* EXPERIENCE.

IT HELPS YOU LOOK AT THE *WORLD* AROUND YOU IN A MORE *CREATIVE* WAY.

IT GETS YOU *ACCUSTOMED* TO WRITING ON A *DAILY BASIS*.

HEY! IT MAY EVEN HELP YOU LEARN SOMETHING ABOUT YOURSELF.

JUST *REMEMBER*, I'LL BE READING THIS, SO ONLY WRITE WHAT YOU DON'T MIND ME *READING*.

THIS WAS GOING TO BE A *PIECE* OF CAKE!

KLICKETY KLICK KLACK KLACKETY KLICK KLICK KLACK KLACKETY KLICK KLICKETY KLACK KLICK KLACK KLICK KLACK KLICK KLACK

I figure if there's one thing I can do, it's express myself. Plus, it's cool that I can actually get school credit for this. I mean, normally when I "express" myself, I just get detention.

And this isn't even all of it. There's much, much more.

Like, Joan was really sorry for the misunderstanding. She swears (SWEARS!) that bumping into Kyle was a coincidence and that she was only at the mall for a few minutes (with her mom) and then went home and spent the night talking on the phone with Pajamaman. Seriously! She says she spends hours on the phone . . . with PAJAMAMAN! How is that possible? I swear, I officially have no idea what's going on anymore.

I think this whole Kyle thing might be frying my brain. Not that there is a Kyle thing.

I mean, yes, he's cute. There's no doubt about that. I really like the way those two little pieces of his hair stick up like bunny ears (or like devil horns, I guess, depending on your point of view). But, look, lots of things are cute. Spider monkeys are cute, that doesn't mean I want to marry a spider monkey, right? Right. So it's the same thing with Kyle. Kyle is just another spider monkey. A spider monkey of loooooove. Agh! Why did I type that?! I don't want my teacher reading that! Especially a teacher that's dating my aunt! As a matter of fact, I don't want ANYONE reading ANY of this.

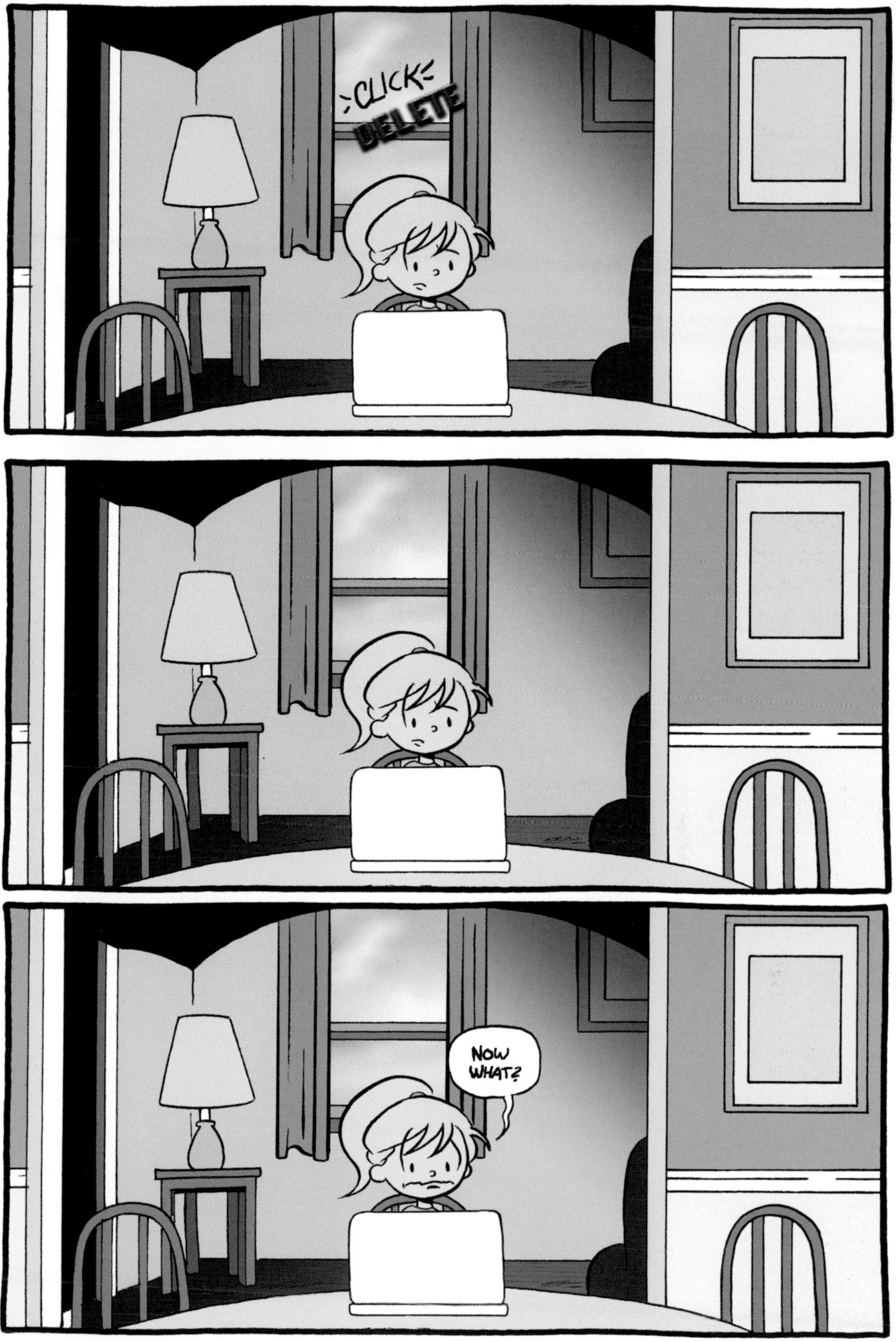
CLICK
DELETE
NOW WHAT?

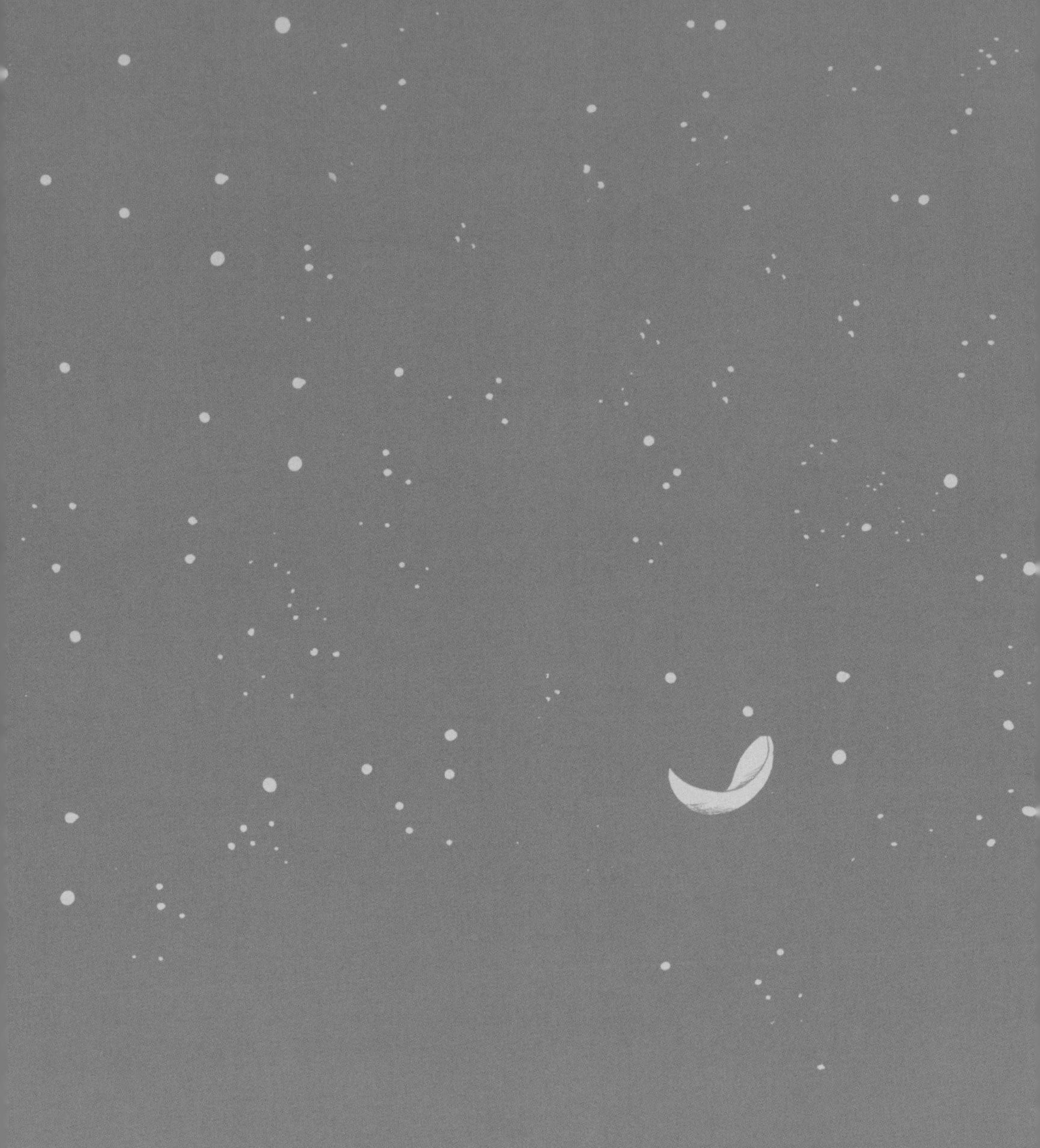

"Growing up is the hardest part of growing up, but what choice do we have?"

-Tanner Clark
in her private journal

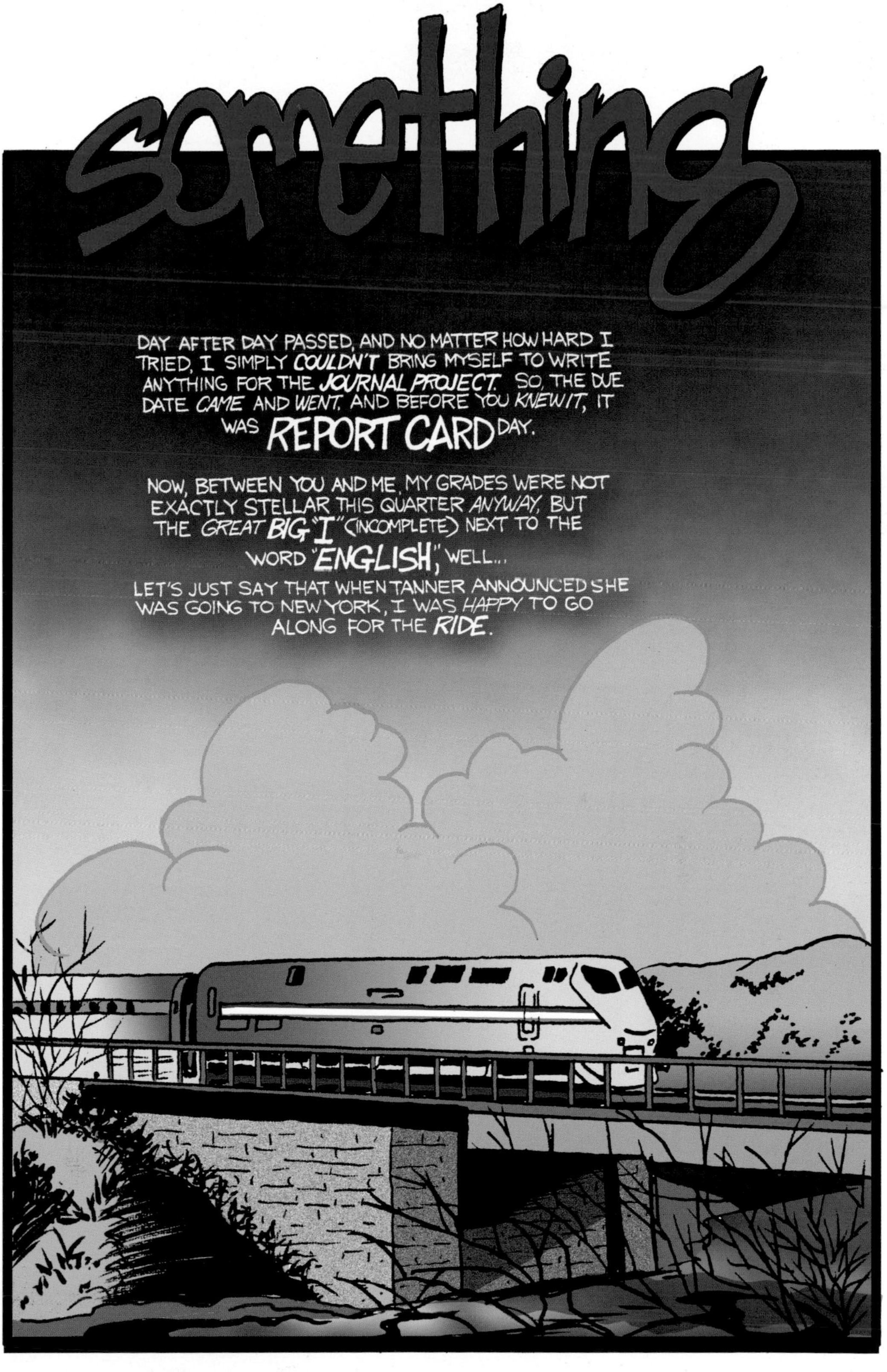
something
DAY AFTER DAY PASSED, AND NO MATTER HOW HARD I TRIED, I SIMPLY COULDN'T BRING MYSELF TO WRITE ANYTHING FOR THE JOURNAL PROJECT. SO, THE DUE DATE CAME AND WENT. AND BEFORE YOU KNEW IT, IT WAS REPORT CARD DAY.
NOW, BETWEEN YOU AND ME, MY GRADES WERE NOT EXACTLY STELLAR THIS QUARTER ANYWAY, BUT THE GREAT BIG "I" (INCOMPLETE) NEXT TO THE WORD "ENGLISH", WELL...
LET'S JUST SAY THAT WHEN TANNER ANNOUNCED SHE WAS GOING TO NEW YORK, I WAS HAPPY TO GO ALONG FOR THE RIDE.

127

128

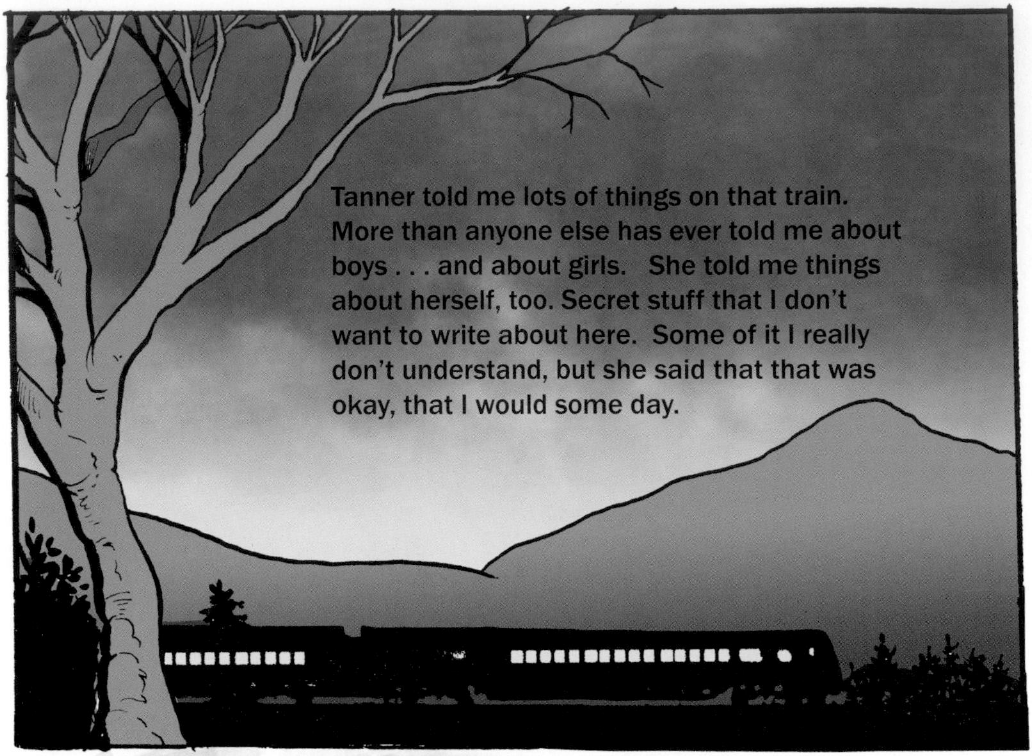
Tanner told me lots of things on that train. More than anyone else has ever told me about boys . . . and about girls. She told me things about herself, too. Secret stuff that I don't want to write about here. Some of it I really don't understand, but she said that that was okay, that I would some day.

She didn't make me feel bad about liking Kyle, but she did tell me to be careful. She wouldn't say anything else, but I don't think she likes him very much. Anyway, I felt a little better by the time the train arrived at Penn Station. My dad had taken the day off, and I was looking forward to seeing him.

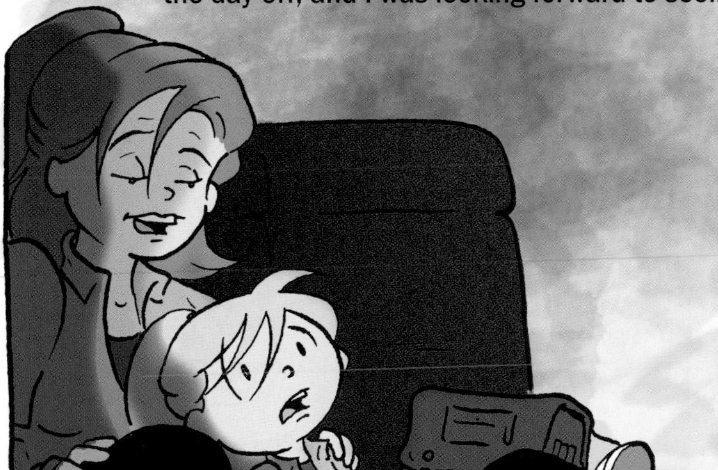

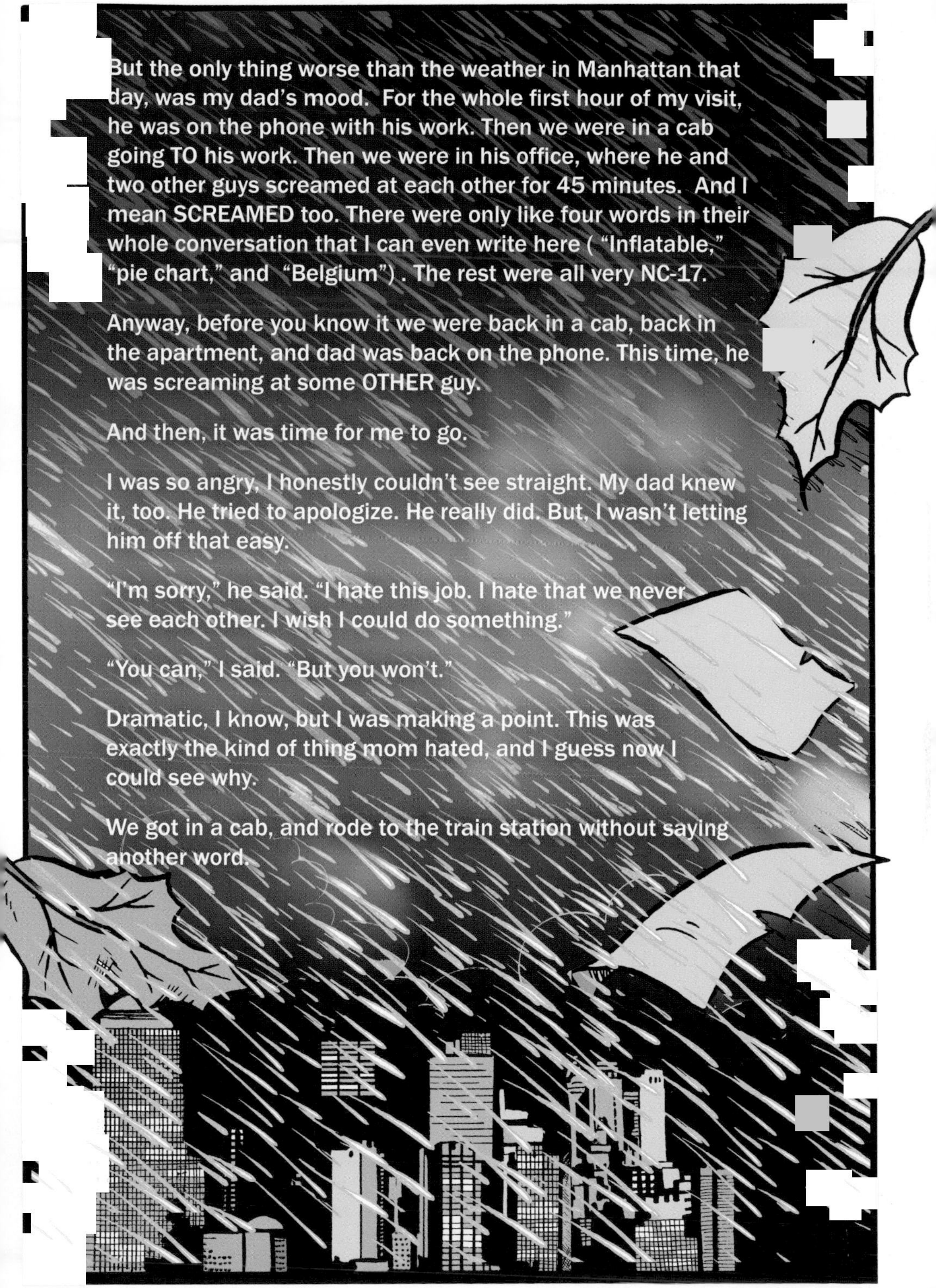

But the only thing worse than the weather in Manhattan that day, was my dad's mood. For the whole first hour of my visit, he was on the phone with his work. Then we were in a cab going TO his work. Then we were in his office, where he and two other guys screamed at each other for 45 minutes. And I mean SCREAMED too. There were only like four words in their whole conversation that I can even write here ("Inflatable," "pie chart," and "Belgium") . The rest were all very NC-17.

Anyway, before you know it we were back in a cab, back in the apartment, and dad was back on the phone. This time, he was screaming at some OTHER guy.

And then, it was time for me to go.

I was so angry, I honestly couldn't see straight. My dad knew it, too. He tried to apologize. He really did. But, I wasn't letting him off that easy.

"I'm sorry," he said. "I hate this job. I hate that we never see each other. I wish I could do something."

"You can," I said. "But you won't."

Dramatic, I know, but I was making a point. This was exactly the kind of thing mom hated, and I guess now I could see why.

We got in a cab, and rode to the train station without saying another word.

Any thoughts I had about complaining to Tanner on the way back died the moment I saw her face.

For the first twenty minutes of the ride home, neither of us spoke. Finally Tanner said, "They didn't want it."

"Want what?" I asked.

"My music." Then she reached into her coat pocket and pulled out an unlabeled CD in a clear plastic case.

"They didn't even listen to it."

I don't really want to write everything that Tanner said, because I think she'd want some of it to be private, but what happened was this:

She wrote a song. My song, the first song she wrote in a long, long time, and it felt good. Then she met a boy. A man, actually. And she liked him. And he encouraged her. So she wrote MORE songs. She didn't have much money, but what she had left, she spent on making a studio for herself. A place where she could write songs, and record them. When she finished five of them, she scheduled a trip to meet with the people who had put out her last record, all those years ago.

It never occurred to her that they wouldn't care.

For the longest time Tanner sat there with her head in her hands. She was crying, but she thought that I couldn't tell. Finally, she looked up and told me not to worry. My mom got her an interview at the place she worked. It was a secretary job. It had nothing to do with music. But it would keep her from losing her house.

"Tanner Clark. Rock-and-roll secretary. Sounds like a musical comedy," she joked.

I laughed. But I didn't feel like laughing.

Eventually, Tanner fell asleep, and I was able to listen to her CD.

It was great.

Of COURSE it was great. It was Tanner.

Since there were only five songs, so I was able to listen to them over and over. Just sitting there, listening, watching her sleep, thinking about everything she has done for me.

I knew what I had to do. I didn't WANT to do it, of course, but I knew I HAD to.

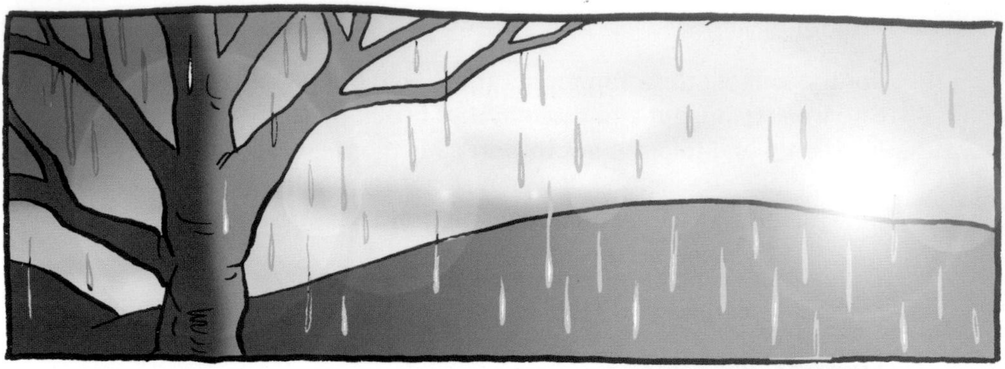

I hadn't been to Joanne Hannigan's house since the day I met her. Back then, the *Tweenie Zeenie* was just a little thing she made on her printer, but now it was a website. Apparently, it was a really, really POPULAR website. Sam still worked with her, but now he was "ART DIRECTOR." That made me laugh. Hannigan couldn't stop bragging. "We have fifty gajillion hits a week. Eleventeen hundred page views per blah, blah, blah."

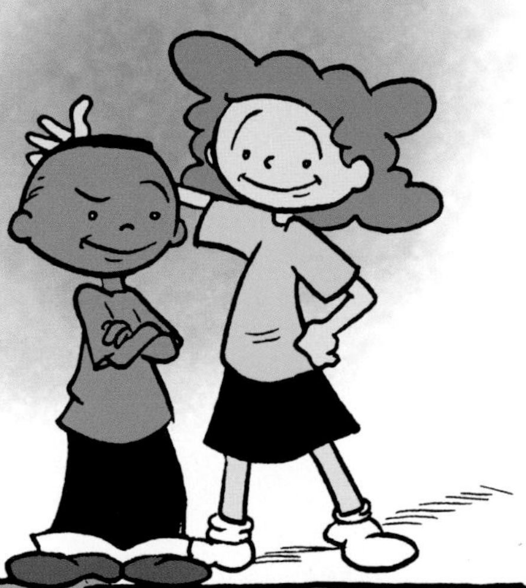

I asked her how so many people ended up downloading Tanner's song.

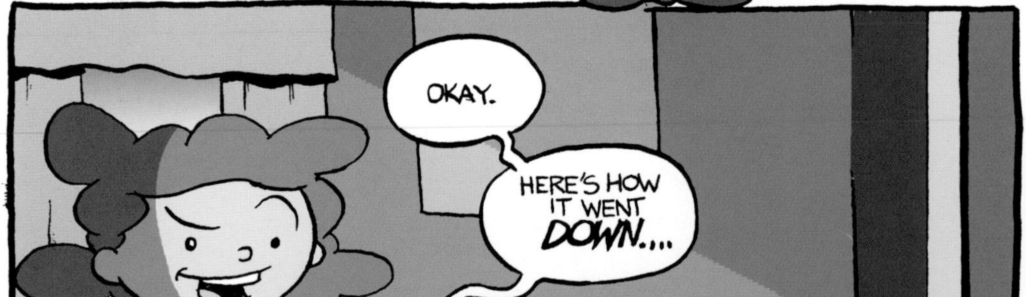
OKAY.
HERE'S HOW IT WENT DOWN....

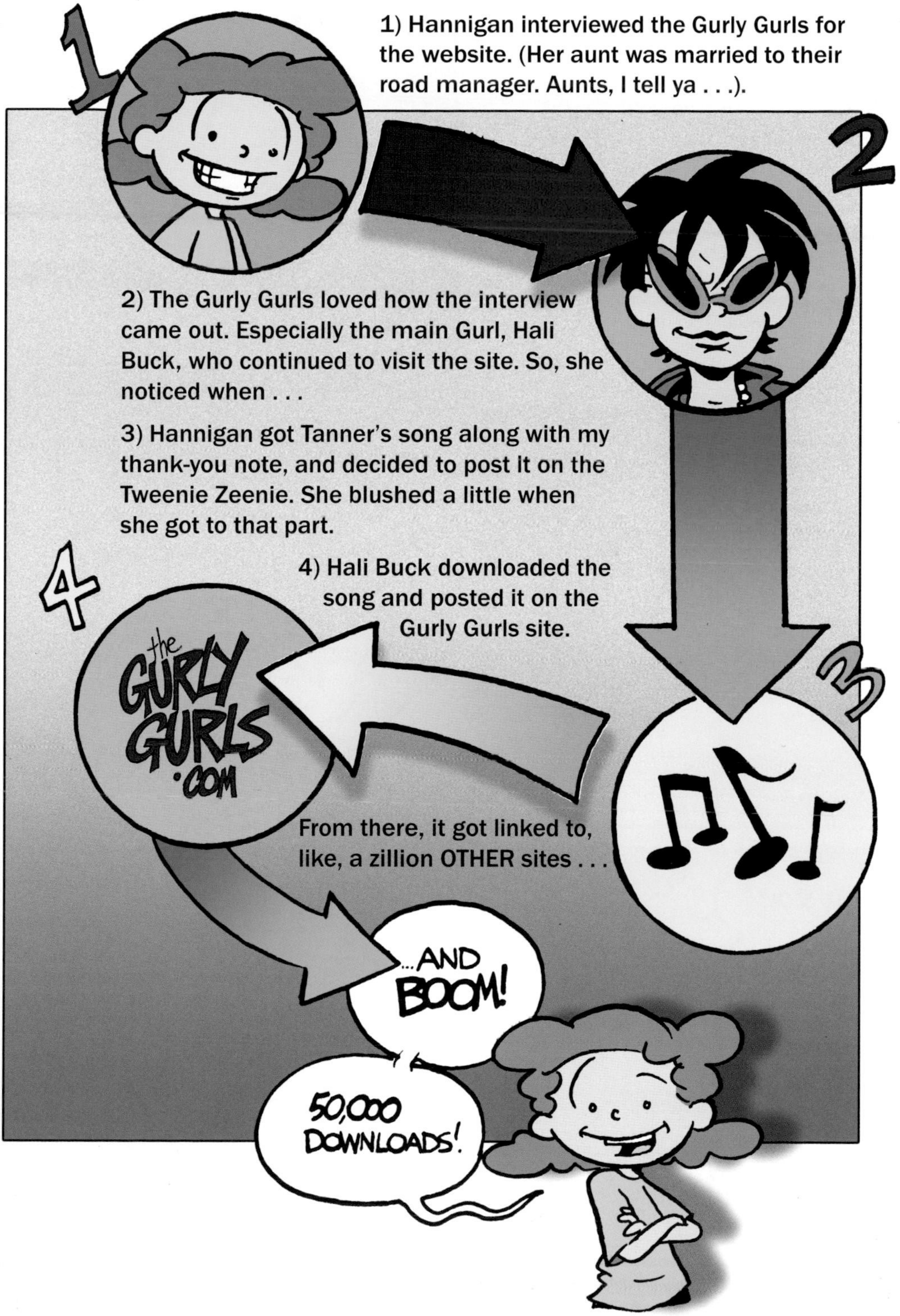
1
1) Hannigan interviewed the Gurly Gurls for the website. (Her aunt was married to their road manager. Aunts, I tell ya . . .).
2
2) The Gurly Gurls loved how the interview came out. Especially the main Gurl, Hali Buck, who continued to visit the site. So, she noticed when . . .
3) Hannigan got Tanner's song along with my thank-you note, and decided to post it on the Tweenie Zeenie. She blushed a little when she got to that part.
4
4) Hali Buck downloaded the song and posted it on the Gurly Gurls site.
3
the GURLY GURLS .COM
From there, it got linked to, like, a zillion OTHER sites . . .
...AND BOOM!
50,000 DOWNLOADS!

Before you knew it, the album was everywhere. Tons of sites were linking to it, people were sharing it, blogging about it, reviewing it. It was crazy.

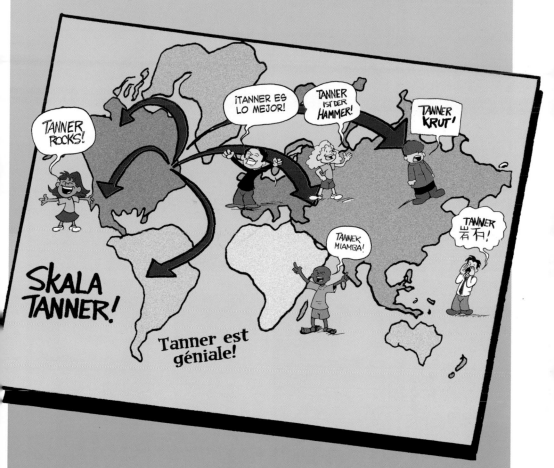

And the whole time, I kept trying to figure out how to tell Tanner that I, let's say, "distributed" her album for her. I didn't want to say anything at first, because I figured she'd be mad. But one day, she came over and said she'd been getting tons of e-mails about her new music. She must've known I was the one who posted it, but she never said a word.

I think she was just happy that people liked the songs. It seemed like that might've been enough.

But a few days later the big bombshell arrived.

The last thing I wanted to do was to tell Tanner to leave, but what could I do? She's always ready to help me, how could I not help her?

It was announced that before the tour kicked off, there would be a bon voyage performance, Tanner AND the Gurly Gurls. So I put the fact that Tanner would be leaving out of my mind by working on one of my other problems. I put on my nice dress (my OTHER nice dress) and went over to Kyle's house.

Over the next week, I didn't see Tanner much at all. She was either with the Gurly Gurls, rehearsing, or with Mr. Henderson.

I made sure all my friends got to go to the show, and I made doubly sure they were in the front row. I got to be backstage, which was AWESOME. From there, I was able watch as the people started filtering in, and eavesdrop as they told one another stories about Tanner's music, and what it meant to them.

I wasn't really surprised when Mom told me Dad couldn't make it. Apparently, he had something more important to do. I *was* surprised by all the signs. So many people showed up with these signs, and banners, and they all had Tanner quotes or lyrics on them.

I guess I wasn't the only one Tanner had been telling true things to over the years.

About ten minutes before showtime, I positioned myself by the entrance. I was starting to get worried that Kyle wasn't coming or that he'd miss me or that somehow security wouldn't let him in.

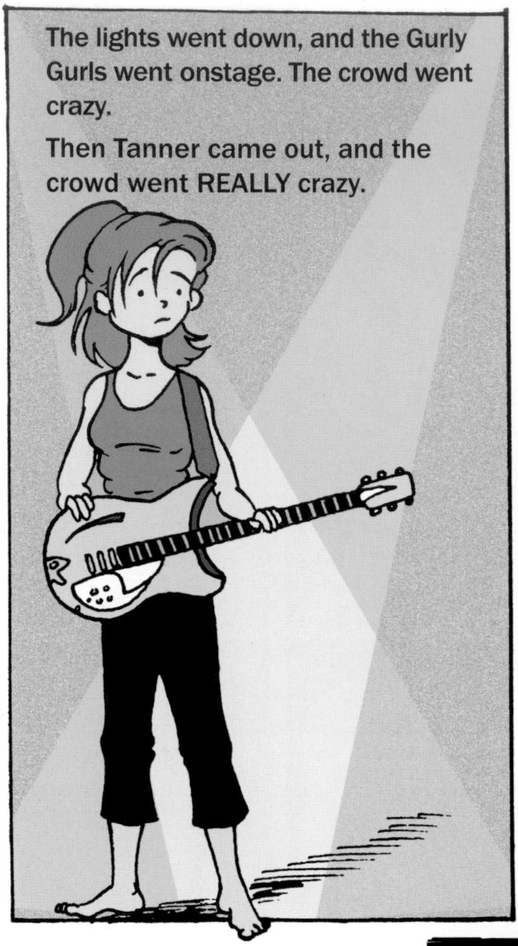
The lights went down, and the Gurly Gurls went onstage. The crowd went crazy.
Then Tanner came out, and the crowd went REALLY crazy.

They kept screaming and yelling, and Tanner kept standing there for what seemed like forever. I thought maybe she was having stage fright or something.

Eventually, the crowd got so loud, I could feel the room vibrate. And then, at just the moment when it seemed like the whole room was going to erupt . . .

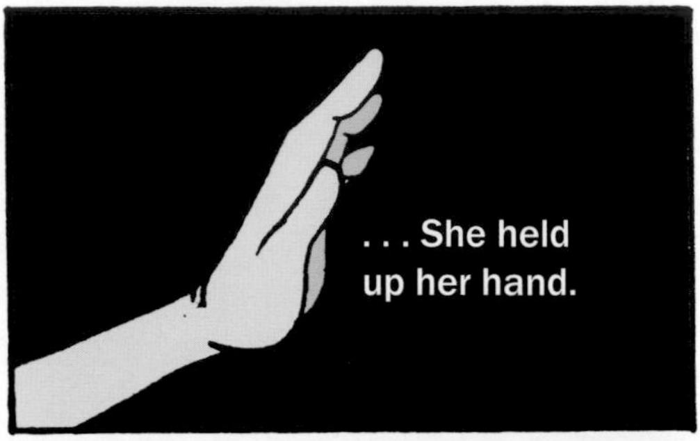
. . . She held up her hand.

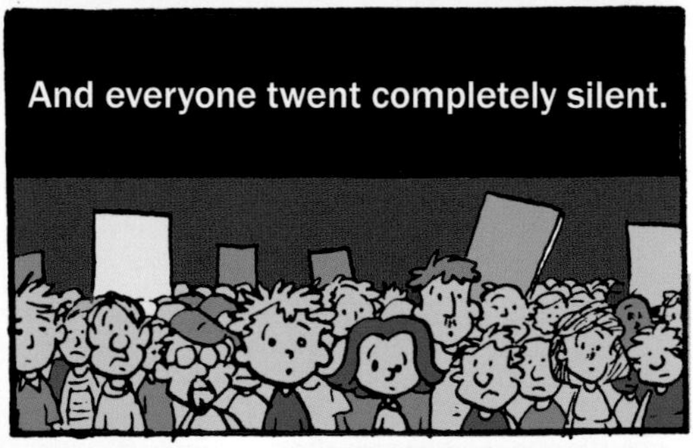
And everyone twent completely silent.

The woman onstage didn't even look like Tanner, anymore.

She was something else.

Then, in the middle of all this quiet, my mom leaned over and whispered in my ear . . .

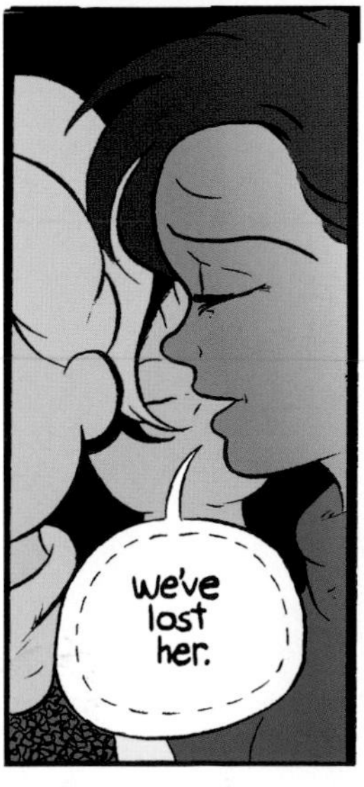
we've lost her.

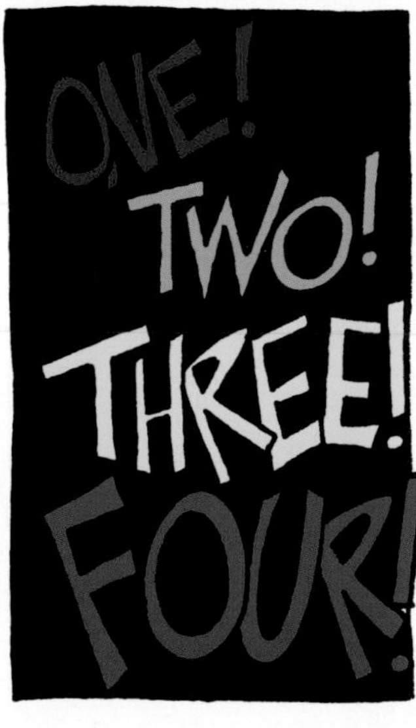
ONE!
TWO!
THREE!
FOUR!

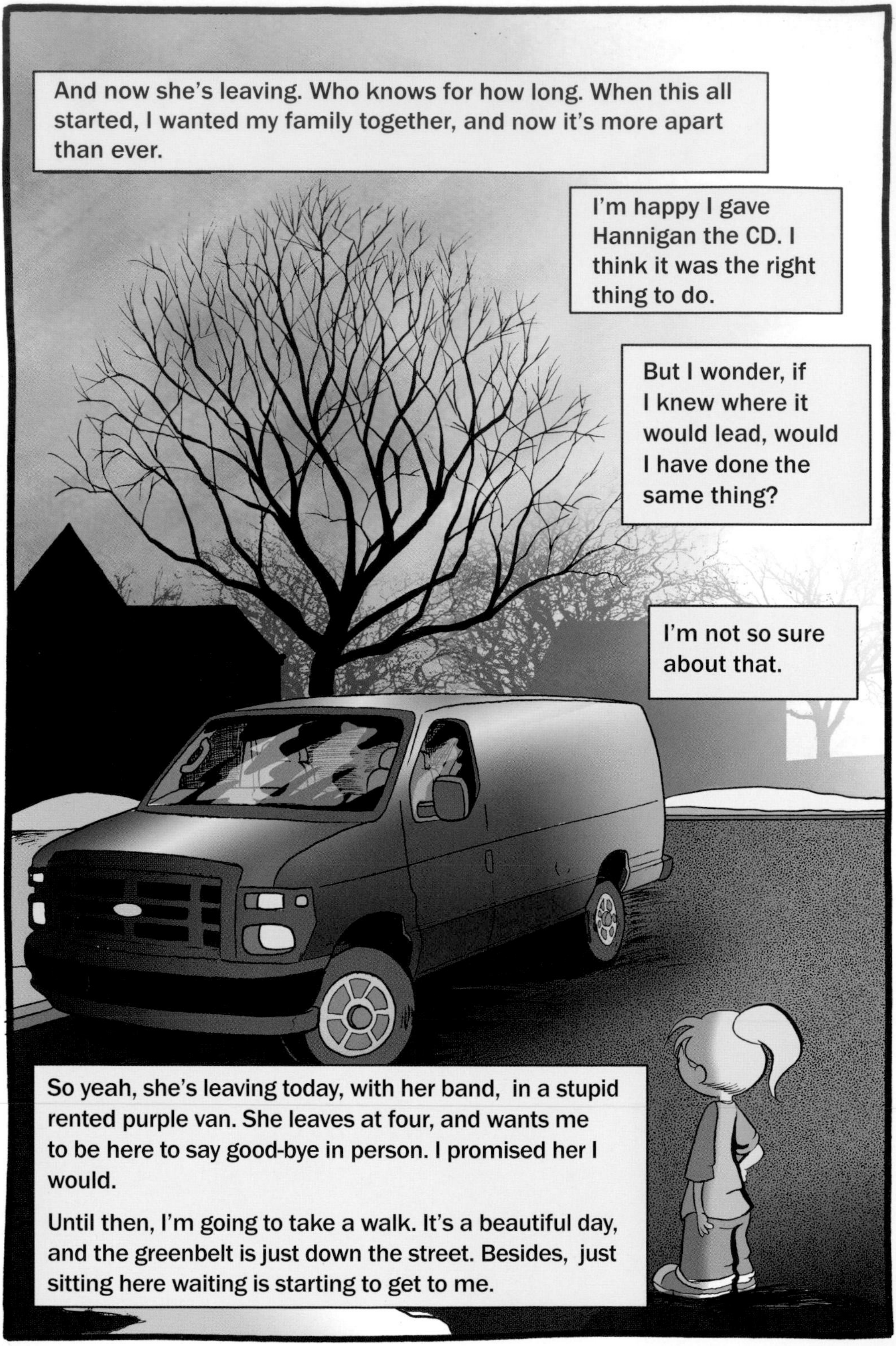
And now she's leaving. Who knows for how long. When this all started, I wanted my family together, and now it's more apart than ever.
I'm happy I gave Hannigan the CD. I think it was the right thing to do.
But I wonder, if I knew where it would lead, would I have done the same thing?
I'm not so sure about that.
So yeah, she's leaving today, with her band, in a stupid rented purple van. She leaves at four, and wants me to be here to say good-bye in person. I promised her I would.
Until then, I'm going to take a walk. It's a beautiful day, and the greenbelt is just down the street. Besides, just sitting here waiting is starting to get to me.

148

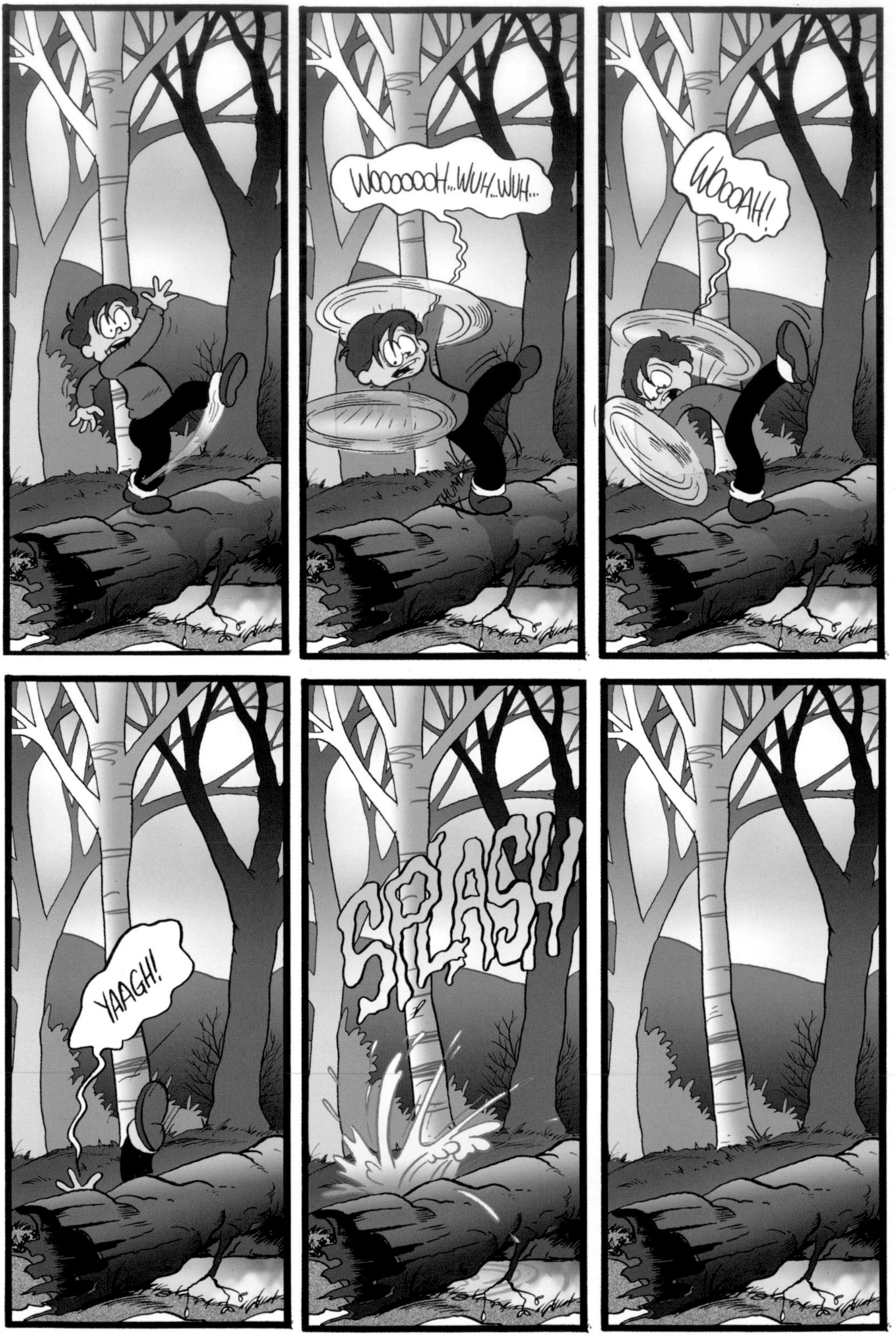
WOOOOOOOH...WUH...WUH...
THUMP
WOOOAH!
YAAGH!
SPLASH

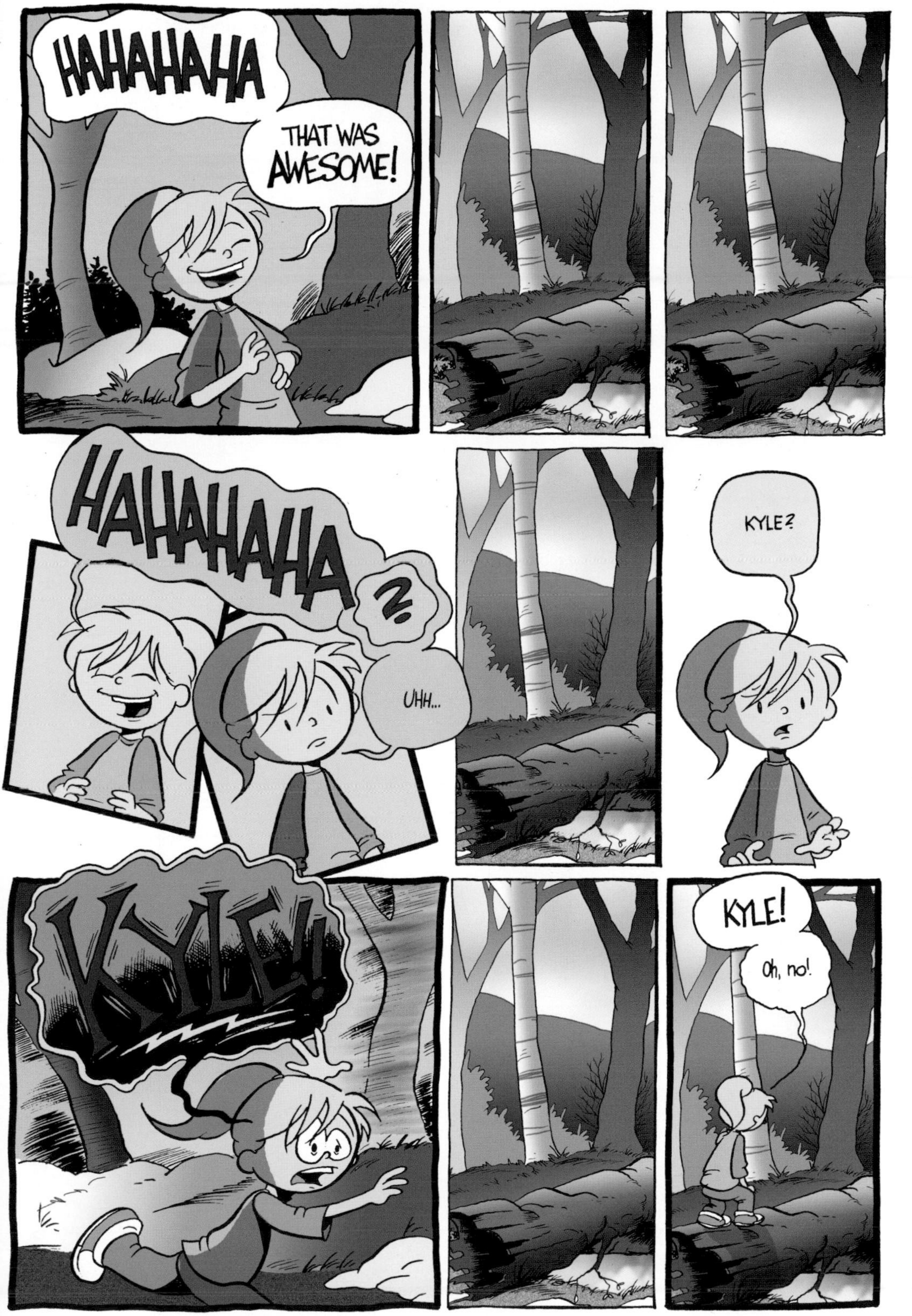
HAHAHAHA
THAT WAS AWESOME!
HAHAHAHA
?
UHH...
KYLE?
KYLE!
KYLE!
Oh, no!

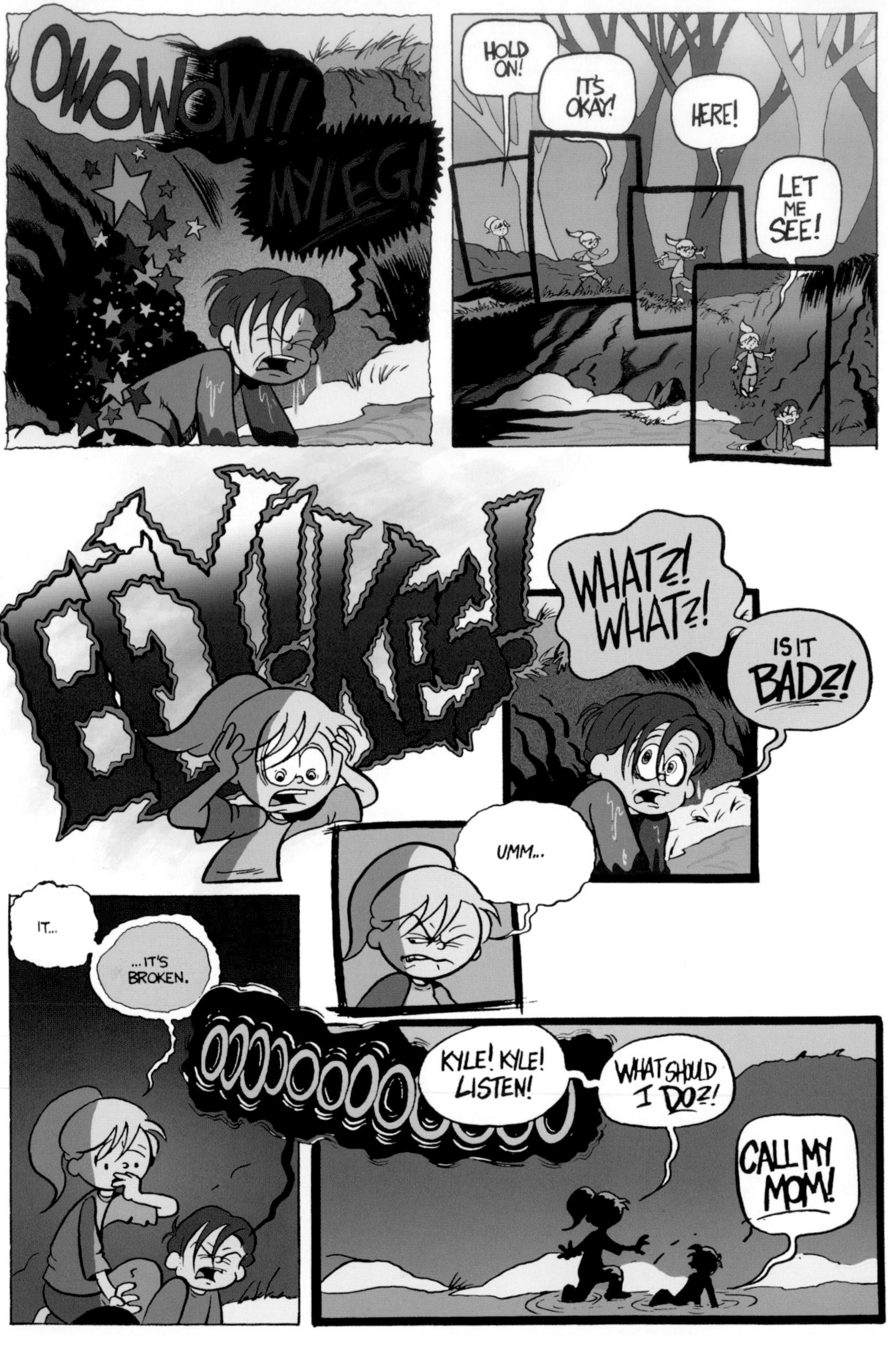
OWOWOW!!
MY LEG!
HOLD ON!
IT'S OKAY!
HERE!
LET ME SEE!
YIKES!
WHAT?! WHAT?!
IS IT BAD?!
UMM...
IT...
...IT'S BROKEN.
OOOOOOOOOOOOOOOO
KYLE! KYLE! LISTEN!
WHAT SHOULD I DO?!
CALL MY MOM!

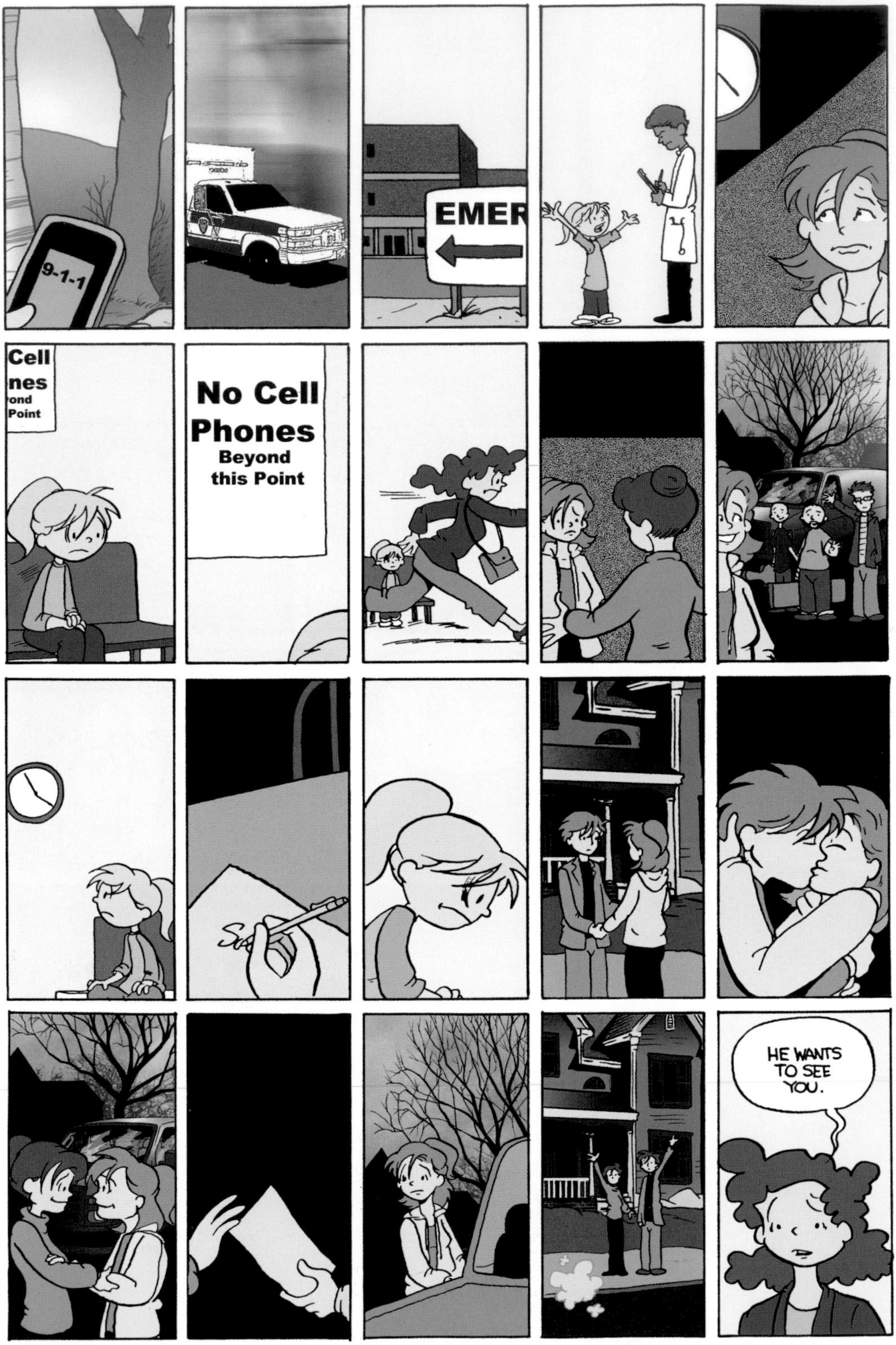
9-1-1
EMER
Cell
nes
ond
Point
No Cell
Phones
Beyond
this Point
HE WANTS TO SEE YOU.

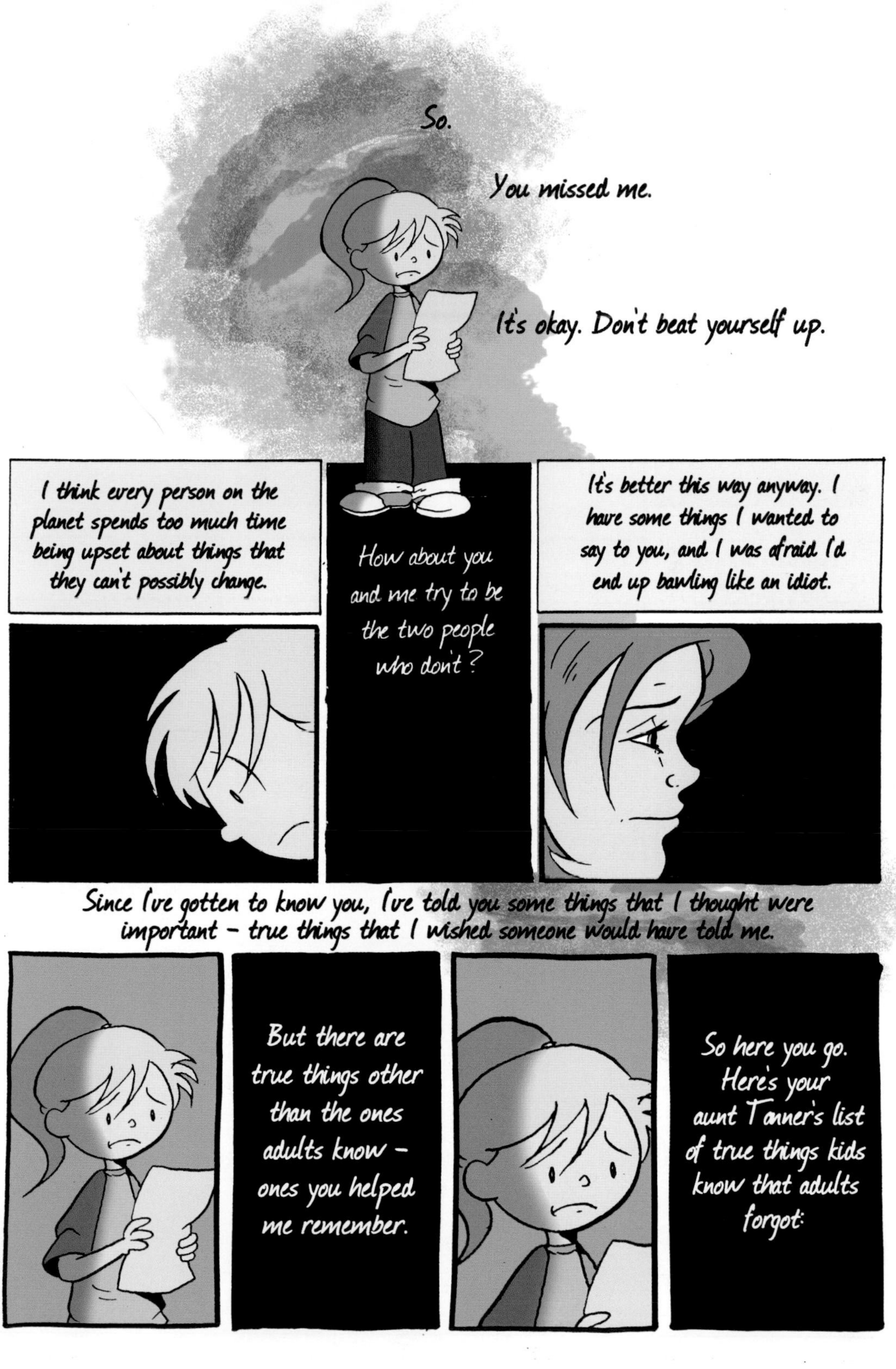
So.
You missed me.
It's okay. Don't beat yourself up.
I think every person on the planet spends too much time being upset about things that they can't possibly change.
How about you and me try to be the two people who don't?
It's better this way anyway. I have some things I wanted to say to you, and I was afraid I'd end up bawling like an idiot.
Since I've gotten to know you, I've told you some things that I thought were important – true things that I wished someone would have told me.
But there are true things other than the ones adults know – ones you helped me remember.
So here you go. Here's your aunt Tanner's list of true things kids know that adults forgot:

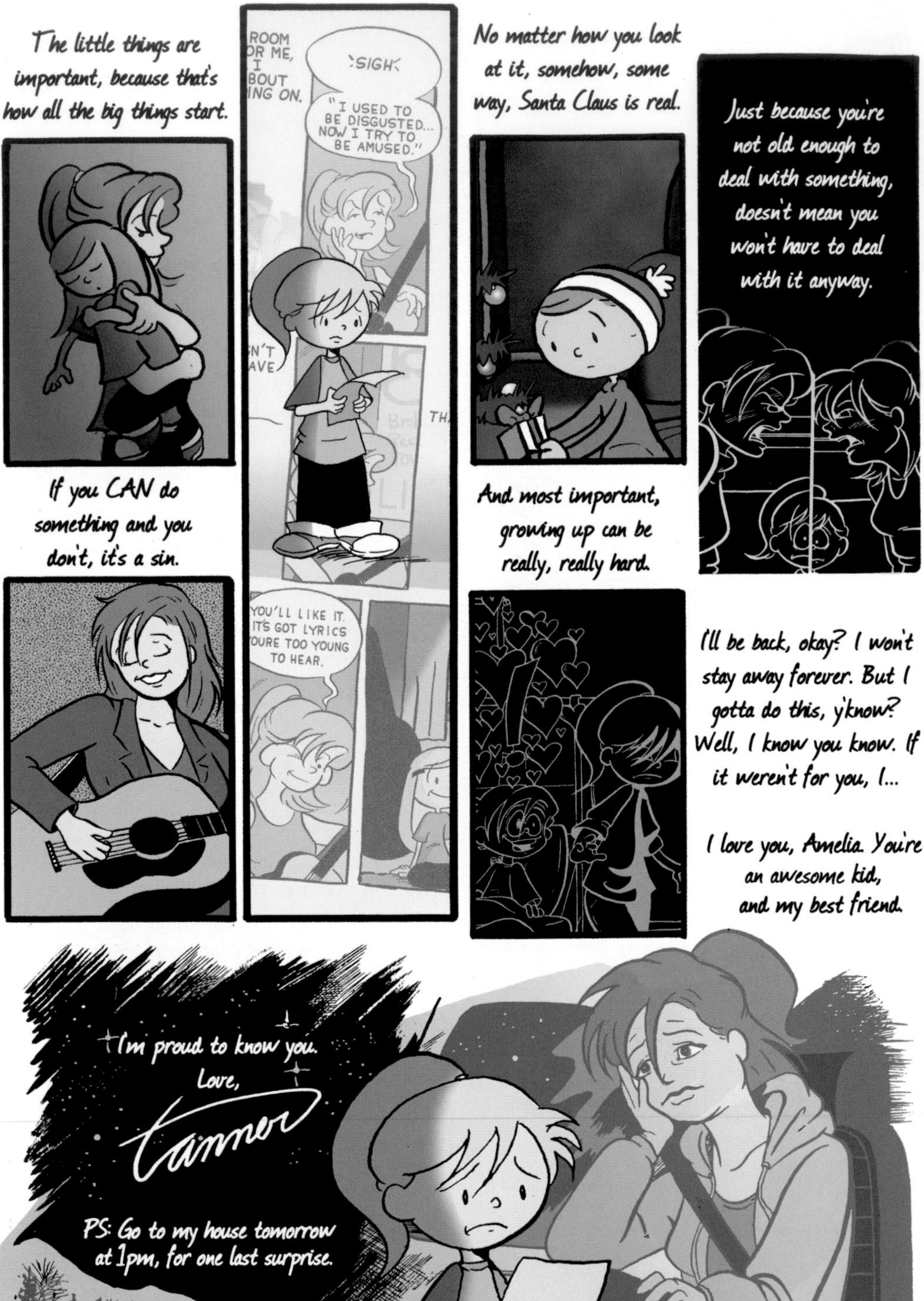
The little things are important, because that's how all the big things start.
SIGH
"I USED TO BE DISGUSTED... NOW I TRY TO BE AMUSED."
No matter how you look at it, somehow, some way, Santa Claus is real.
Just because you're not old enough to deal with something, doesn't mean you won't have to deal with it anyway.
If you CAN do something and you don't, it's a sin.
YOU'LL LIKE IT. IT'S GOT LYRICS OURE TOO YOUNG TO HEAR.
And most important, growing up can be really, really hard.
I'll be back, okay? I won't stay away forever. But I gotta do this, y'know? Well, I know you know. If it weren't for you, I...
I love you, Amelia. You're an awesome kid, and my best friend.
I'm proud to know you.
Love,
Tanner
PS: Go to my house tomorrow at 1pm, for one last surprise.

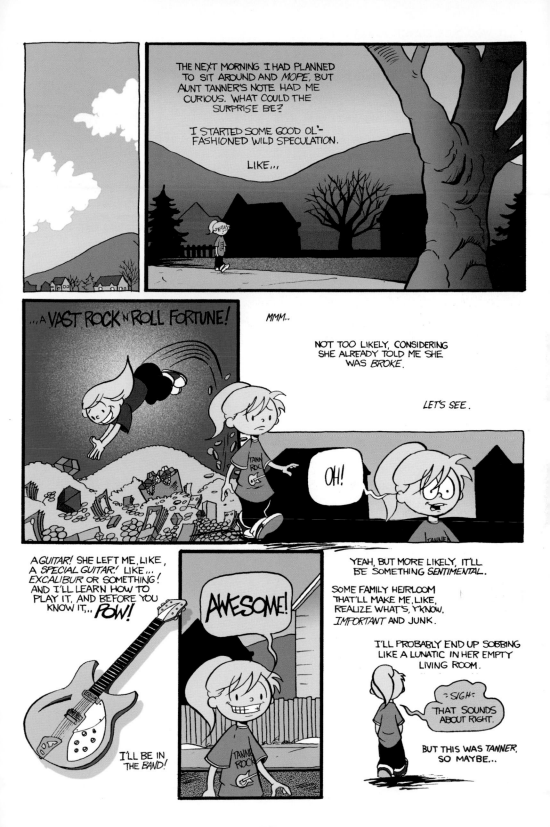

...IT WOULD BE SOMETHING *PERFECT.*

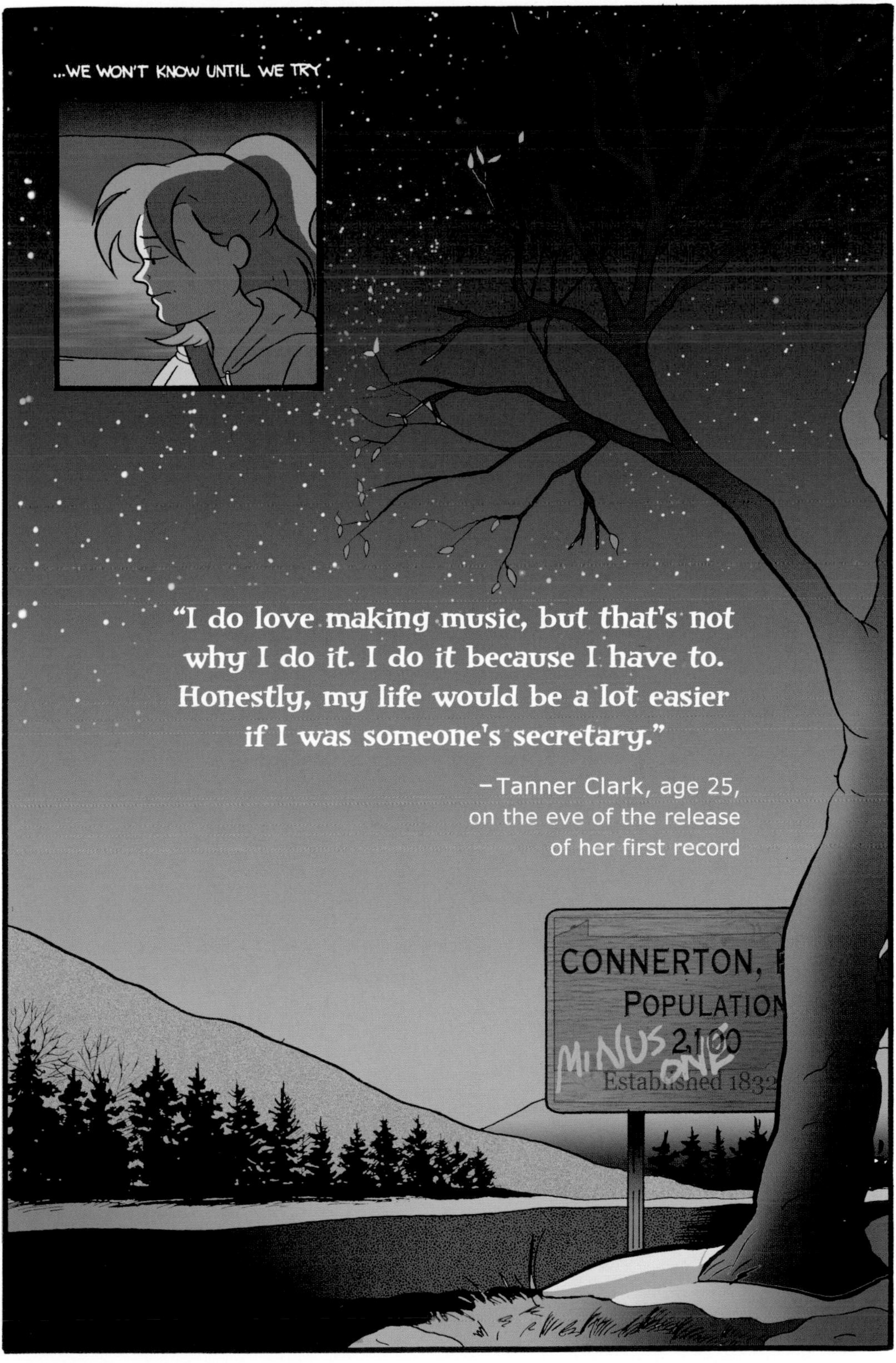
...WE WON'T KNOW UNTIL WE TRY
"I do love making music, but that's not why I do it. I do it because I have to. Honestly, my life would be a lot easier if I was someone's secretary."
–Tanner Clark, age 25, on the eve of the release of her first record
CONNERTON,
POPULATION
2,100
MINUS ONE
Established 1832